MODELO  ANTIGUO

MODELO ANTIGUO

A Novel of Mexico City

BY

LUIS·EDUARDO·REYES

TRANSLATED BY Sharon Franco & Joe Hayes

Cinco Puntos Press
El Paso, Texas

Originally published in Spanish as *Modelo Antiguo*.
© 1992 Ediciones Era S. A. de C. V.
Calle del Trabajo 31, 14269 México, D. F.

Modelo Antiguo, A Novel of Mexico City. Translation copyright © 1997
by Sharon Franco and Joe Hayes.

FIRST EDITION

Library of Congress Cataloging-in-Publication Data

Reyes, Luis Eduardo, 1958-
[Modelo antiguo. English]
Modelo antiguo: a novel of Mexico City / by Luis
Eduardo Reyes; translated by Sharon Franco and Joe Hayes.
p. cm.
ISBN 0-938317-32-6 (paper)
I. Franco, Sharon, 1946-. II. Hayes, Joe. III. Title.
PQ7298.28.E934M613   1997
863—dc21
97-28170
CIP

Cover art, Lowrider, *1976 Copyright © 1997 by Luis Jimenez.
Thanks, Luis!*

Thanks to Bill Verner for turning us on to this wonderful novel!

Cover and book design by Vicki Trego Hill of El Paso, Texas.

*This book is funded in part by
generous support from*

FIDEICOMISO PARA LA
CULTURA
MEXICO/USA
THE ROCKEFELLER FOUNDATION ◆ FUNDACION CULTURAL BANCOMER
FONDO NACIONAL PARA LA CULTURA Y LAS ARTES

PART ONE

Holy Saturday

1

What Were You Doing Around There?

LAST NIGHT I had a dream which I forgot when I woke up. But the feeling it provoked has stayed with me—or I should say, the NON-feeling. It was as though I were without life, suspended in the void, waiting for something definitive. No, it wasn't for death, dear Diary; rather, I was waiting for what might have been the fulfillment of a promise made long ago and forgotten. I wasn't thinking of who had made me the promise; that was not at all important. What was essential was that I be open to that enigmatic possibility...

THE LIGHT turned green and I was about to take off when suddenly I saw her there, standing in front of the windshield.

At first I didn't think or feel anything, I just sat there like an idiot. Then she crossed the street. I saw her walk down the avenue like she didn't know where to go. She met up with a street walker and stopped cold. And then something really weird happened because when she stopped it was like all the movement of the street stopped with her. It was just as if some giant had posed us all there to take a picture from up above. But it just lasted for an instant, because then everyone went merrily on their way again like nothing had happened. A guy walked up to the whore. The woman looked away from them; she moved a couple of steps back and then took off out of there, almost running, with little bitty steps like a bird. That was the first time I thought that she was crazy, that her nerves canceled out her age and turned her into a child.

She went on until she met up with some guys in black tennis shoes, high tops laced up tight, with wrinkled leather jackets, reeking like fifteen- and sixteen-year olds. Their hair was sticking out all over the place and they were muttering curses she didn't understand. All she did was pick up her pace. The three pairs of tennis shoes tried to follow noiselessly, but the laughter and the puddle-splashing gave them away.

The night got darker. She came to a corner and waited for a taxi. She tried to flag one down but it drove on by. The three guys moved closer to her. I put the car in first; she motioned to me and I started to drive away too, but then I braked after a few meters. *Okay, just one last fare, to pay for dinner.* I had stopped about twenty paces away from her, but she made it in ten and got in. Silence.

It seemed to me that her breath blotted out the outside world, except for the black tennis shoes multiplied over and over in the bright drops of the last rain of an ordinary Saturday. That's how I met her.

"Where to?" I said.

I had to wait a while until she finally said, "To Santa María de la Ribera."

"De?" Why did she add the "de" when it was just Santa María "la" Ribera? No doubt about it: a crazy old bat.

We drove away leaving everything as it was. I watched her in the rearview mirror. She was still nervous. I stared at her mouth because she was moving it almost incessantly, muttering God-knows-what crazy bullshit.

"What did you say?"

She stopped moving. Her lips too.

"What?"

"I asked what you said."

"I don't understand…"

I smiled.

"Forget it. It's not important."

I kept watching her open mouth in the mirror. It was moving less; she was calmer.

"You feel better now?"

That made her wary. Then she was off again, talking to herself without saying anything.

"Excuse me for sticking my nose in your business, but you were so…out of it when you got in. It's dangerous. It's real dangerous to be out walking the streets at this hour. Don't you think?"

She bit her lower lip while she thought about what to answer.

"We never know…"

Ay, he keeps talking, she was saying to herself.

"…what day, what time we're going to get it. We live with Jesus in our mouths…"

Now he's brought God into this. I read the words in the agitation of her mouth.

"…although some of us don't even remember the Our Father who art on Earth."

That must have gotten to her because finally she said, "That's an outrage."

That was all she said, but just like that, so sure of herself. To me, of course, it didn't mean a damn thing. But what about this bossy tone of hers? Wasn't she the one who had just been scared shitless?

"Go into any church and they'll teach it to you again," she said when I thought she wasn't going to say anything else. Her tone pissed me off.

"Ugh! I can't even remember the last time I went to a church."

And much less when he went in, her lips said silently.

I laughed right out loud as I replied, practically spelling the words out for her:

"Don't…ask…me…now…when…was…the…last…time…I…went…into…a…church."

She froze. She must have been asking herself how I could guess what she had only said in her mind. Who was I? A magician? Her fate in the form of a taxi? The Devil! She didn't want to be frightened any more; she'd had enough with the black tennis shoes and the petrified hair.

She shut her mouth and sat there like a locked box. Her eyes were suspicious: *He just better not take any side streets off the Circuito Interior.* I don't know what got into me to make me keep fucking with her.

"Now that I think about it…"

My God, I wish I could close my ears, her face said again.

"…I haven't had a single customer who has asked me to take him to a church. Nobody goes any more, do they? And I've been in this business a long time, señora."

"Señora!" The word rolled around in her head and fell like a bus token toward her crotch. Then she looked like she was about to open up wide and pour out a whole flood of words, but for some reason she didn't do it. She probably thought it wasn't worth arguing the point with someone she wasn't ever going to see again.

"So you go to church?"

She didn't answer. She was seething. I asked her again two more times; and then she answered in a nice tone. Real nice, real polite, you know. And that was all, that softened me up.

"Okay, pardon me. It's obvious that you're the real thing, a respectable woman, not that I go around picking up any old slut that…"

"Please!" she said.

Later I would learn that when that old bitch said "Please," it meant "That's enough!" It meant "Shut up. I've had just about all I can take of you!" In short, it meant a whole shitload of things.

Then, absolute silence until we arrived.

"Here it is."

I parked the taxi in front of a small, narrow house. Nothing out of the ordinary. Yellow, with a garage. None of the fancy porfirismo touches. The other day a guy, a passenger, had pointed some out to me when I'd been in the same neighborhood. One window on the street and a door like all the others.

"How much do I owe you?"

"Let's say ten, okay?"

She paid exact change. She moved away from my VW bug and I heard her little steps moving toward the house.

What made her stop? Search me. *Something's going on with that mummy*, I thought.

She walked back slowly, like she was going to have me take her some place else, and then she poked her head though the window and asked me if I had a friend who might like to work for her. As a chauffeur. So that's what she wanted, a driver. No, I told her. Not that I can think of. Sorry.

"Well, if by chance you hear of someone, tell him to come to this address… I hope it will be soon." And she handed me a little slip of paper where she'd written the street and the number.

Then she did go into her house. And disappeared.

I put the car in gear and left.

2

What Was the Deal?
Why Me?

THE NIGHT was thickening in its own broth. *That's it, everything's cool; now it's time to get some rest… No, I think I'll get a cup of coffee first.*

There was a café I liked in the Hipódromo district, even though it was more expensive. I was beginning to get a taste for the good life. It was really fine to feel like all those sons of bitches who have it all given to them on a silver platter. With the tables on the sidewalk, like they say they have in Europe. So what if it was only the Hipódromo? It was good enough for me.

Tacos and coffee, my late night snack. It was cold out, no doubt about it.

Between bites of tacos and sips of coffee, I thought about something: I'd had it up to here with the life of a taxi driver. Any way you looked at it, being an old lady's chauffeur wasn't such a bad deal. And the rest of the time you could be driving around picking up the servant girls, or the servant girls who lived next door to the servant girls; that didn't sound so bad, did it?

And maybe one day they would order me to drive them to the outskirts of town and that would be my salvation. I was dying in this fucking city. *Bitch of a town: she breaks every bone in your body but won't ever leave you alone.* But no, what are you thinking of? Nothing but dumb ass fantasies... I wonder what her daughters are like? Shit, by now they've got to be grown women too. And what about her granddaughters? No, they've got their own wheels. I'm sure the old lady wants me just for herself. Fine, that's no problem. All of this I was chewing over in my head as I drank my coffee.

Suddenly a black car stopped right in front of me with the brights on so I couldn't even see what kind it was. I gulped down the last of the coffee. I covered my eyes. My dark skin turned neon white. The goddamn light passed through my hand leaving no shadow. With the same hand I gestured to the waiter, but as I was asking for the check the horn started blowing and you couldn't hear a thing.

"What? What did you say? I can't hear you," the waiter shouted.

"Bring me the check," and I made the sign of writing in the air; even in China everyone knows what that means.

"Two thousand five hundred."

"What?"

"Two thousand five hundred pesos."

"Can't hear you. I wish that son of a bitch would shut up."

"What?"

I was no longer paying attention with my ears, but I was with my eyes. I watched the waiter's mouth and that's how I found out what I had to pay. He gave me change, I left him a tip. Adiós. And at the same time the noise ended.

As I was walking away I turned to look at the black car, and it blinded me again because it had shifted a little bit towards me, but without any sound from the engine, I swear. I stood there, shading my eyes with my hands. I stared at the beam that was lighting up that little piece of night. A fucking chill raced up and down my spine; then right away it was gone. Turning my back on the light, I went into the darkness where my taxi was.

As I drove to my house in the Estrella district, I kept thinking about that car. It was really weird. I felt like someone—or actually, that car—had singled me out, as if it had chosen me from among many. What was the deal? Why me? And it had even moved all by itself to keep the light on me.

At the same time, Barbara was at the window of her house looking and looking—supposedly at the smoggy sky—but really like thinking of me, you know? Real romantic. Later she confessed that she had "mysteriously" known what happened to me that night. I remember that I got mad at her then and hollered at her not to go around acting like a goddamn psychic with me.

I went into the kitchen to see what there was to eat; I was still hungry. It was always like that with those European-style places in the Hipódromo.

Everything was a godawful mess, strewn around between the two filthy pieces of furniture that made up my living room and dining room. I was taking the ham out of the broken glass case, my fridge, when I saw the slip of paper with the old lady's address. I left it there. The damn ham tasted bitter and I took it out of my mouth and tossed it all chewed up onto the paper. Then I went to bed; I laid on my back looking up at the ceiling and before I knew it, I was catching flies.

By morning, the pillow had told me what to do. The ham was totally rotten and the little piece of paper was soaked in stinking grease.

And now what? The battery was out in the Volks. Goddamn it. I had to find some other way to get to the Santa María district.

By the time I got to her street, it was already afternoon. A Holy Saturday for me, all right. I kept looking at the slip of paper with the address on it, but I couldn't remember where the house was. The numbers skipped around, and houses were missing which probably had never even existed. The only thing that was clear was that I was in the odd numbers and the address was in the evens. I crossed the street and at that moment an old, old car, all done up for a wedding, almost wiped me out.

Damned if I knew where that fucking paper went, gone with that car. Well, anyway, the house was around there some place. And I finally did find it, after going around the block twice. I knocked and something moved behind the curtain. No time to see what it was. The door opened and she appeared. It was daytime and she looked, I don't know, different. She was less dried up. Even young, if you didn't look carefully, and considering that she had to be around fifty-five or sixty years old.

"I came to see about…"

"Yes, I know, come in."

"What the…you already know ?

"You're here about the chauffeur's job, right?"

I freaked out big time. She was already calling me "tú," acting real buddy buddy. Here was this woman again, standing in front of me, and me like a fucking imbecile once more. Finally I managed to think, *Well, I'll just check it out. If not, I always have the taxi; it just needs a battery… What the hell*, I thought at last, and then said, "Yes, as a matter of fact, that's why I came."

She didn't say anything more. She turned around and her backside motioned for me to come in. I looked her over from head to foot— so what if she was old? I wouldn't be a man if I didn't.

I didn't have time to wonder why someone who looked so poor would need a driver. I did that later. We went into the garage and holy shit! I saw the car.

"Listen, that's the same one that almost ran me…!"

"Yes, this is it. Come into the living room, please," she interrupted.

She hadn't understood that it was the same car that a second ago had almost run me over. I stood there expecting who knows what, and she had to come back to get me.

The living room: a bunch of dusty paintings and some funky old-fashioned furniture. Nothing to steal, too bad. But anyway there I was.

"Look, I couldn't find anyone who wanted to be your chauffeur and I said to myself, Well, I could do it. That is, of course, if it's all right with you." She didn't answer. Locked up tight again. "I have experience, as a taxi driver, I mean. As a chauffeur, no, but it can't be too hard. I know how to drive and I know my way around the city, what else is there...right?" She said nothing. "Uh...maybe you're thinking that I made up my mind too quickly, and that's be..."

"I've got to have a chauffeur. I'm fatally ill and I wish to die in my car somewhere around here."

She had to tell me twice before I got it into my head. No, she wasn't crazy, not much. She was just totally off the wall, ready for a padded cell! My body didn't respond. It took me a while to stand up. My mouth was already salivating around the curse I was going to spit at her, but suddenly my lips turned to starch and I only said, "What? What kind of little game is this, anyway?"

"It's no game." She stood up to take hold of my shoulders and sit me down again. "Life never gave me anything, not a single wish, not one solitary unreality. Magic was denied me. Then not long ago I realized that I was being granted just one right: to choose where I would die. In this alone am I privileged."

Shit! Is she playing with me? Well, I can get into that. And no one's quicker on the uptake than me. That's why I went along with her.

"You don't say. And what are you dying of?"

"That's none of your business."

"Even if you're making me part of your death?"

"That's exactly why not: whose death is it, anyway, yours or mine?"

"Well, yours, of course, thank God."

She was right. Death was her thing, not mine. Much later I found that out, but at that moment how could I have guessed it when I was just getting to know her? I felt bad, as if she'd been making fun of me.

"And since I don't have time for dumb stuff like this, with your permission, ma'am, nice to meet you and I'll see you later." I ended very properly.

She sat there. Not me. But on my way out, even with the creaking when I opened the door, I could hear clearly how she was trying to talk me into it.

"The car will be yours when I die. It will be soon, I can promise you that. But if you accept, I'll need you full time."

Slowly I sat down again next to her.

"You could sell it for a good price or keep it, I don't care. That's your business. The only condition is your time, as I already told you."

I looked in her eyes, but I didn't learn anything more because I don't know how to read eyes. The mouth I do. For me the mouth is most important because that's where the soul comes out. I know them all and I know when they're lying or when they're horny, soft and moist, asking to be bitten; or when they're thinking hard; or when they reveal the horror of an impossible forgetting. I looked at her mouth, but with her I wasn't sure if she was telling the truth or not. Well, how could I be, if she was out of her mind?

"Don't you think you're going a little too far?"

"I know what you're getting at. Don't worry about your salary. I'm going to sell everything: the furniture, some jewels and clothing I no longer use."

"You don't mean the house too?"

"No, because it's not mine. I'm renting it. I have for a long time, you know, but it doesn't interest me any more. I almost never go out and lately I'm starting to hate it. Well, what do you say?"

Only to herself did she say her real motives. And to myself I mumbled, *Crazy old woman.*

I stood up and without saying goodbye I went out through the garage. A word to the wise, they say—you know what I mean. But, shit! there was the Ford. What was I going to do? It was so beautiful! So incredibly fine! She came up behind me on silky feet. I didn't even hear her and I jumped when she said, "Here"—she gave me the keys— "and here's three hundred thousand pesos to get the car fixed up. I want them to do a good job on it. We'll be traveling constantly. I'll see you in a week. In the meantime, I'll take care of everything."

She took the ribbons and bows off the car just like it was a humongous black present. She opened the door for me real graciously and I slid into the ship of lost memories. It was as easy as that. There's something about those old cars that the young ones just don't have.

"Turn it on," she ordered.

I couldn't do it and I was afraid she would fire me. But with a smile she told me to release the security lock (a stupid-ass little lever underneath the fucking seat).

"Now try it."

She closed the door.

"Will you tell me your name or do you prefer for me to call you Jaime?"

"Juan."

"Well, welcome, Juan. I'm Barbara Somethingorother. I'll expect you in a week. Not one day later, do you hear?"

LIFE HAS TRICKS to keep you from dying the day before. That's why we don't notice things; we're not even aware of them when they're happening to us. Now, like about a thousand years later, I know that right then and there I could have died of happiness.

3

Modelo Antiguo

I TOOK the car out. It was a black ribbon that I waved around her house a few times, to see if she was spying on me or anything. *Agh, that old bag is such a...* Then I forgot about her and left.

A new car even though it was old. I was happy. I didn't start believing it until about twenty stoplights later. I drank it in with my eyes. I wrapped it around me. It was mine, and to boot I had three hundred thousand pesos to celebrate with.

At a stoplight I remembered that they had already started putting radios in old cars like that. When I turned it on, out came the crackly sound of a swing tune from the forties, maybe from the same year the car was made. And then something happened that I still don't understand. The old lady had said something about magic or some such thing, and I think the idea stuck with me; so much happening in such a short time. Could she be a witch? My fate in the Santa María? The Devil's grandma! Damn! Okay, first I'm stopped at a light, right? (on one of those old streets); then I turn towards a store from way back when grandma was a girl, with old fashioned Coca-Cola signs with the soda turned all green, and then I see two old guys that almost seemed to have popped out of the trunk, with vests and sombreros of the same faded gray you see in those old portraits.

They looked at me, smoking cigarettes without filters.

They were laughing and making fun of me. There was no doubt about it. They were walking arm in arm. It wasn't a dream, I swear to God. Suddenly I hear an ad on the radio, one of the ones they have on now, and in a flash I'm back in the present; the people on the street were from the present too. Little by little my breathing calmed down, and a little later, I did too. I could still see the old men—they were disappearing into the sunny glare of the wall across the street— but their laughter would follow me into the future. Forever. I put the car in second without realizing it and drove off gulping gasoline.

From the window of my house I could see the Ford parked across the sidewalk. It wasn't in bad shape. Neither was the owner of the car. How could she have given it to me just like that, without even knowing me? It just didn't make any sense. To be so trusting! Now me, I wouldn't even trust my own mother that much, and she's six feet under ground. I was thinking all of this out loud.

"What's this? When did you start talking to yourself?" Laura said.

"Now we have a car for the wedding."

"Are you going to start singing that old song again?"

"I don't get it. All the other chicks are dying to get married and you're just the opposite."

"It's like I already told you. It's not that you don't turn me on; I'd sweep the street with my eyelashes for you, I won't deny it. But you know what, Juan?" She gave me a hug, pressing her body against mine. "I really have no desire to be married. My ex left me totally traumatized. If you only knew what a drag it is. You only want it because you haven't been there, that's why. Just give me a little room to breathe, okay? To see how I feel, you know?"

She was talking from the heart, and that's why I understood her. I was in love with her and what could I do? It happens like that some- times with a passenger: the rear-view mirror at a certain angle, and her at another; from first to third I was undressing her, and by fourth gear she was my old lady.

"Okay, if you want, we'll forget about the wedding, but even so, let's get started on the honeymoon."

She sat right down on top of me with her legs open.

"Oh, baby, come on. We've even burped up the wedding cake."

I HELPED HER into the old car.

"Why won't you tell me where you got this thing, huh?"

"Just luck, I guess."

"But luck's a stranger around your house."

"That's what you say."

She was better educated than me and I never had the right words to answer her back. But she was teaching me some. She was a teacher. And for my part, I taught her how to read lips, so that after a while we could communicate in silence.

"Okay, so where are we going?"

"To do the town, even if it's only once in our lives. Look, I've got what it takes to love you right."

I waved the wad of bills in front of her nose and that kept her quiet, like when I first got to know her from Pino Suárez to Portillo.

"Well, let's get on with it; I have classes to teach tomorrow morning."

"No way, tonight we're going to party till the sun comes up—to celebrate. And then we're going to celebrate each other, right?

"Celebrate each other?"

I moved my lips and right then she felt the heat. She gave me a shove. "Damn you, don't you ever get enough?"

"No, not when what I want is to give it to you, pinche Laura."

Once again with my lips I told her that I was crazy about her legs, and with my tongue I moistened the message. Laura caught fire like dry grass.

"Don't talk about it so much, just show me."

The Ford was fine for fucking.

The car was as obedient as Aladdin's black genie. It took me from here to there and back again; it did everything that had to be done; it stopped when it should have stopped and moved wherever I felt like going. First backwards and then forwards; now to the right and now to the left. Until we ran out of gas.

We ended up dripping with sweat, semen and grease. The windows were so steamed up we couldn't see out of them.

I don't remember when I dropped Laura off, because I went on partying with the car.

I woke up with my mouth pressed against the horn.

"Shit, what's with you? Why are you making such a racket?" I said to the Ford, because without even meaning to, I was already getting into the crazy habit of talking to the car. I couldn't find any cigarettes, much less any money. I'd somehow managed to blow all that cash in exactly one week.

"That's it, tomorrow I'm selling you. I'll take whatever I can get." I also thought that maybe one of these days I could even go back to driving the taxi, and act like nothing had happened. Then I got mad at the car. Then at the old lady. And in the end at myself. My head ached.

I felt pretty damn sad.

"Listen, really, what if I try to get some more money out of the old bitch? She already wants to die, right? As far as I can see, she's all alone in this world... But just watch, I'm going to keep her company. I mean, unless you got any objections."

I dragged myself out of the car and started cleaning it with my shirt (shining away a week's worth of puke stains). And right in the middle of this, I fell back asleep on the hood, with my arms wide open, like I was comforting it.

4

From on High

IT'S A LIE: I'm not happy. Nobody can be. Inside our bones before we die we are still whatever we were meant to be even before we were born... Once again the knife blade of guilt cuts its way through my heart. And I cry in silence my bitterest tears."

The next day was the end of the week she'd given me, and there was the Ford right in front of her house: clean. She could open the door without being afraid of catching some disease. It was just like new, although the engine still hadn't been worked on. I was acting all cool and collected. Barbara came out giving orders.

"I'm ready now. Put those packages in the trunk. Not that one; we're going to need it. There are two suitcases in the entry way. Put them in the trunk too."

Then she went to one of the back doors and waited there. I stood at attention, like a candy-ass soldier boy. She stood stiff as a board too. Neither one of us moved. How long was this going to last? The poor old bitch didn't know what the hell was going on. What was she waiting for? What was the problem?

I looked at her mouth to find out, but no. I lifted my eyes and followed her gaze to the back door. Finally I caught on and opened it. It's easier to understand what to do when people tell you, no?

Now I was a chauffeur. I loaded the stuff in the car and then I took my place at the wheel. Silence. Then she practically hollered, "Let's go!"

Okay, let's go. Without asking her where to, I pulled out. We said adiós to the Santa María district. Who knows what she must have felt at this first goodbye?

I got tired after half an hour of driving around aimlessly.

"You still haven't told me where you want me to take you."

She came up with something off the top of her head. "Let's see, park over there in front of that restaurant."

I stopped the car right by the Ciudadela plaza.

"Bring the package," she said, kind of mysteriously.

She chose a table way in the back, near the rest room. She looked at me and I lowered my gaze to her lips, but they were pressed tightly together like with hatred. I would have traded what I know about the mouth for what I don't know about the eyes.

She raised her eyebrows.

"Are you going to sit here?" she said, like it was something outrageous, like I was pulling my pants down right there in public.

"What?"

"You shouldn't say, 'What?' You should say, 'I beg your pardon?'"

I swallowed my anger with a mouthful of saliva.

"Okay, then, I beg your pardon?"

"I asked if you were going to sit here."

"I don't know… Can't I do that, or what?"

"It's not that you can't do it, it's that you shouldn't do it."

"And so…?"

"Do I have to tell you why you shouldn't?"

I kept quiet, and I guess that was like saying yes.

"As far as I know, ladies don't eat breakfast with their chauffeurs. Remember that, if you please."

"Oh!"

¡Pinche vieja hija de su chingada madre, ruca de mierda! I wish you would drop dead right on the spot.

"Why don't you say anything? Didn't I make myself clear?"

I gave her a dirty look and went and sat at another table near hers.

The waiter treated us the same. I ordered what she did, even though I don't like salads and all those weeds, but I did it so she'd know that I eat the same and shit the same as her. I even ordered coffee. I forgot that I was her chauffeur and just sat thinking about Laura. Before long Barbara called me over to sit at her table. I stood there without moving, real proper. She insisted. I just stood there. She said, Please, and only then did I sit down.

"And what do you want now?" I said coldly.

"Open the package."

"What?"

"You shouldn't say, 'What?' Say 'I beg your pardon?'"

"Why do you want me to open the package?"

"You'll see."

With this woman, anything was possible. Maybe it would be another little surprise like that car. I opened it and found a grey suit with a matching cap with gold stripes.

"It's your uniform."

"What?"

"It's going to be very difficult to teach you to speak. 'I beg your pardon?' You must say, 'I beg your pardon, I beg your pardon, I beg your pardon.' Don't you understand?"

"All right, I get it. Jesus!"

"Good, that's settled. This is your uniform and I want you to put it on."

"There was nothing about a uniform in the deal."

"Put it on."

"No, I'm just fine like this."

"Please."

"Really, thanks, but it's not necessary."

"You're my chauffeur."

"Right, and so when I open the door for you, that'll make it obvious, no?"

"The way you look is the way people treat you."

"Yeah, that's what I'm afraid of."

Some of the people around us were beginning to stare; I could hear murmurs and a few giggles behind me. Again she ordered me to put it on.

"Can't we drop this for right now? Don't you see that people are staring at us?" I whispered to her.

At least she lowered her voice too when she answered me. "So obey me then."

"Look, it would be much better to discuss all this work stuff in private, don't you think?"

That bitch was so stubborn!

"Okay, okay. I'll put it on in the car."

"In front of me?"

She nailed me with a look and I had no choice. I took the package and went into the rest room.

¡Pinchísima vieja del diablo! With her, my manliness just shriveled up.

One of the other customers followed me in just to watch me change. I began with the pants while Barbara was out there paying the check. Then the white shirt. *I hope no one notices me.* The guy who came in after me was grinning, pretending he was washing his hands while he watched me, with his head lowered and cocked to one side. I put the jacket on. The suit was real fine and without the cap no one would suspect a thing. But I put the cap on. With her there was no getting around it: I was a chauffeur. Fuck it. I walked to the door. Before I closed it, I turned and flipped that jerk off.

Of course, there was no way in hell people weren't going to notice me. I could hear them laughing all around me and I felt their eyes like fucking mosquitos digging into me from every direction. Barbara pretended to be sitting in some other world, but I was watching for one smirk out of her, and my ass would be gone. Just one. There it was! One little twitch of a smile. I practically ran out of the place and Barbara threw the tip on the table. I got into the car and turned on the ignition. She came running like crazy and jumped into the front seat, next to me.

"Listen, what's the matter with you?"—*¡Enchiladas!*—"I'm talking to you."—*¡Iguanas!*—"You almost left me hanging from the door! I am not going to tolerate these outbursts from you, so if you want to keep your job, you better watch what you do! And now…Stop …Stop!"

"Sure, right this minute." And I put on the brakes hard. Her eyes popped out of her head when she saw the windshield coming toward her. She took a deep breath, just one. Then she sat up again, like nothing had happened; she got out of the car, as straight as you please, and got in again in the back, all proper and lady-like.

"Let's go."

I took off again laying rubber, keeping an eye on her lips, which I could see reflected in the rearview mirror in front of me. *One more shitty little smile and I'm going to crash*, I thought. But the old lady held it all in. Who knows how she managed to do it? At times she was really good at keeping things hidden behind her face.

To my right, I could see her topple over when I swerved left to pull into a gas station.

Okay, I got gas and we took off. As we were driving, she asked, "How much was it?"

"Thirty-five thousand."

"And the receipt?"

Motherfucker!

And so I went right back, but when I made a U turn, I almost smashed her against the side window.

I gave her the fucking receipt for the goddamn gasoline. Maybe now she'd stop jerking me around. But no. In the middle of the block, she crumpled it up into a little ball and threw it onto the floor of the car. Now I was totally pissed off.

"What are you muttering about, Juan?"

"Nothing. I'm making myself a promise…boss."

"And may I ask what that might be?"

"I'm going to work hard so I can get married."

"Oh, you have a girlfriend!" she said to me, like she was talking to a three-year-old kid.

"Uh-huh."

"And what's your girlfriend's name, Juan?"

Stupid! I thought, but I said, "Laura."

"I promise you that you'll have enough for your wedding with Laura."

What an old pain in the ass! Never before had I wished for the death of a passenger, but this time I begged God himself for it with all my heart.

"Oh, it's wonderful that there are still men in the world who think like that! A wedding in white, in the church, just as God wills it."

Please let her die. Please let her die.

"I'm pleased that a boy like you still thinks about getting married."

"Okay, okay. Now where to? I'm tired of driving up and down Bucareli."

"Too bad—I'm not."

I took a deep breath and counted to fifty, which is higher than they recommend on television. I tried to change her mind. I wasted my breath for nothing. She was rooted like a weed to those goddamn streets.

She was still going on about the same thing.

"Maybe some day you'll introduce me to your girlfriend."

"No!"

I parked the car. Now I couldn't see her in the mirror any more.

"Why not?"

"Because...she's not in Mexico City," I came up with.

"What a shame!"

She was gazing out idly at the street. Her eyes scanned from one side to the other while her head remained still.

"Where are we going?"

"Where do you take your girlfriend at this hour?" she asked me.

To bed. "To the movies."

"No, I don't feel like being shut up in a theater."

Who'd asked her to, anyway? That's the last thing I'd care to do. They say that old chickens make good broth, but for me, no thanks!

"So where to then?"

"I'd like to look at the city from a tall building."

"So let's go to the Latino tower."

"No. When I was young, my father..." That was the first time she slipped up; she got all tongue tied and lost her proper ways. "Daddy used to work. Nearby. His office. And from the window, I..." Then she pulled herself together. Now she was happy, like she was fifteen years old: "I only like things when I look at them from up high!"

"And where is that?"

She gave me directions until we got to a building behind the Palace of Fine Arts. The earthquake had sucked out its insides, leaving nothing but a shell there, toppled halfway into the street.

Anyhow the old lady went in and watched the clouds scraping against the jagged edges of the ruins. Poor fool: not even when she was a kid did those patches of sky seem so blue.

I stayed outside waiting for her. It was at that hour when the city explodes. If at the best of times she kicks our ass, at that hour no one stands a chance, she blows us all to hell. Won't she ever get tired of beating us all day every day? What does she want? Can't she let up? Why doesn't she just finish us off once and for all and put us out of our misery? But no, she does it little by little, by hunger, by exhaustion, by the air, one day by earthquake, fucking bitch! You'd think she'd get bored as hell, never meeting anyone to match her. Tell me, why doesn't she pick on someone her own size? Oh, yeah? IT'S BECAUSE WE DON'T MAKE THE BITCH BEHAVE! Is that it? Is she deaf, or blind, or what? Goddamn rotten whore!

THERE ARE LITTLE MOMENTS, late at night, when she seems to sigh in her sleep. I've sometimes seen her curled up in the Zócalo, in the early hours before dawn. I wonder where she goes when she dreams? And you think, man, how awesome this city is, so high up, you know? Who could have put her here, up on the world's rooftop, where you can see everything down below, so tiny: the wars, what they say on TV, you know, all the countries, AIDS, the moon, all those advances... All that down there, way off in the distance. Me, I can't even imagine what it's like anywhere else. Here we're a bunch of poor sons of bitches, but at least we're right up at the top, high up. I think that's why she gets some respect. Because everyone really does respect her. Well, of course, the ricos—who else?— have some influence on her—money makes the world go round, no?— but when all is said and done, it seems to me that they're hurting too. You couldn't possibly feel like this in any other place, so life's got to be worse somewhere else...or maybe it's better, or, shit, what the hell do I know? When you come right down to it, I just can't imagine being anywhere else... Man, she's just snoring so sweetly, smelling like something red and wet—she's so goddamn big!—rocked by whatever wind happens to be blowing, mending her heart in her sleep so that she can wake up and go right on eating us alive tomorrow. At night only the cathedral keeps its eyes open, it's wide awake. It's too scared to sleep. And then there's also the Palace of Fine Arts and the Post Office and the famous statue of the Caballito that I like a lot because it makes me laugh. And all of those places live in fear of their lives: they know that whenever she wants to, she can roll right over them and wipe them out… But I like her, can you believe it? Because she's for real, and even though she may kill us, she won't ever just leave us alone. My mean-ass old lady!

THE HORNS were honking full blast, splitting my head apart. The ruined building lurched and began to whirl like crazy, spinning round and round me. I covered my ears and closed my eyes. But I couldn't shut out that awful pounding: it was like my heart, in desperation, was beating the shit out of itself.

I don't know how, but the old lady got herself moving, because I saw her come out and close the door of the building, very slowly and carefully, as if she was putting away for safekeeping the disaster of the clouds, to take out and look at later.

"What's the matter, Juan?"

"The noise," I said softly to myself so she could just barely hear me.

5

Scenic Overlooks
of the City

SHE TOOK ME to the scenic overlook on the highway to Cuernavaca. The smog filled me to the gizzard, but it was better than the noise. "This is better, isn't it?"

"Even if it is, I've had it with this city."

A lot she cared. She talked about how in the old days the young couples in love used to go to these places. Especially at night, like right now. I interrupted her because she was getting started with her stories again.

"We could head out on the highway. Visit some other places. I'm from here, but I don't want to die in Mexico City. How about Querétaro? Or maybe one of these times even San Miguel de Allende?"

"No."

"Well, why not? Don't you think it would be great to die in...?"

The headlights looked at me and almost turned on. She didn't even bother to look at me.

"It has to be in this city. No one knows in what neighborhood, street, corner or house their time will come, although I can assure you the place has been set since the beginning of time. It's all the same to me where it happens, just so long as it's in the city I love. You have to understand, Juan, it's the only luxury I'll know in this life. And besides, it gives me a jump on death."

"Not much of one. We're traveling by car, and death flies."

"Don't be an idiot."

Coming from her, insults just sounded stupid and didn't hurt anybody. Finally she had to admit that death travels faster than a '37 Ford.

Now all the talk about how she was going to die soon seemed true to me. *Should I believe her or not?* I thought about asking her right to her face, but I didn't dare. If I were to ask the question the next day, in the middle of the traffic, it wouldn't sound the same. I might not even do it. Things said in the daytime sound lighter; it's like they evaporate. At night things sink in and you've got no choice but to believe them.

And then all of a sudden I'm opening my big mouth, now that I wasn't even thinking of the question.

"Are you really going to…?"

"Really."

I think this business of her death was starting to hurt her.

"When?"

I didn't mean any harm by saying that. I just wanted to be prepared.

"I don't know," she answered shortly.

"And from what?"

She never shared that secret with me, no matter how much I swore I would keep it.

"I swear to you in the name of this city that I'll never tell anyone."

But no way. I didn't understand why she was so close-mouthed either, but anyway I liked her that way because silence is the coolest thing in this world. But there was something mysterious about it.

"Huh?… What are you sick with?…huh, señora?"

"Señorita!"

Oh, my God! No way she could keep quiet about that, and she screamed it in my face to be sure I understood she was a virgin. Though she really did look like one, of course. It was something I still had to find out about... Or maybe it wasn't true that she was a virgin or that she was going to die. *She's putting me on.* That could be it too. I couldn't figure anything out because she wasn't muttering any more. And then she said something that sounded like a promise.

"Maybe one of these evenings, when I'm not fully aware of what I'm doing, the old memories will make me say more than is prudent for me to say."

All that was pretty strange. And then a car came around the curve and filled our eyes with light. I remembered that business with the car when I was in the café. Again I felt like I'd been singled out for something or other. I told her that. "Why me? Why not someone else?"

"Because you wanted it," she answered.

She never asked me where I was from, or my full name, or if I'd ever killed anyone, or if I wanted to rob her. Nothing. She didn't care who I was. All she cared about was that I knew how to drive.

Then she put on her bossy tone again and ordered me to drive us to a hotel in the Centro. I thought a full-time job meant eight hours. What an idiot I was! It did me no good to argue about it; she insisted, and that was it... Fine, end of story!

I opened the car door, but only the wind got in. She was a few steps away, lit up by the lights of the city and she had turned to salt, like the Bible says. I stood there like a dipshit looking at her face, turned upward, white, open to receive something that was obviously making her very happy, with her eyes half closed, almost smiling, like the way they paint the saints when God is talking to them. It's got to be like they're getting screwed by God, right? Later on I found out she was acting like that because at that moment the voice of her Spanish mother was sounding above her head.

"Look at the city! Quiet at last. It looks like it tried so hard to fall asleep that it ended up dying."

"No, Mamá. It's alive because it's not ours anymore. Don't you remember that you took it with you?"

I really heard that.

And then she went on like that, smiling lightly, looking upward. A lot of time must have gone by. I realized it when my body started to ache from standing there so long without moving.

"You ready?" I brought her back from wherever she was.

"I'm coming. We have time. What's the hurry?"

"I hate to bother you, but I really have to go home."

"Don't worry. Remember this is a full-time job, even though it's not for the rest of your life. You'll see how fast the days will go by with me. Think of them as a vacation. You'll come out ahead. I know what I'm talking about."

"But that wasn't the deal we made." And I started insisting again on an eight-hour day.

Not a chance. We climbed into the Ford and left the panorama— to shrink it and tuck it away in our memories. We landed on a huge avenue, brown, treeless, full of people, as always.

6

The Devil's Words

"HERE WE GO AGAIN!" I said.

I seemed to be tied to her, to the smog, to the noisy traffic. It was bad for me and I told her so: my ears were very delicate. A good quality, not a defect, though it depended on the situation. I told her that I had been driving a taxi here and there for more than seven years. The cab didn't belong to me. I was sick of it. I didn't tell her this, but I had thought that maybe as a chauffeur I'd do better, and it was worse, actually, I don't have to tell you. I had already thought of it and I remembered it again. Things came into my head for a second and even a third time. I think she was the reason for this. It wasn't like that before. I used to live only for the moment—whatever came my way, with no before or after. I didn't know how to remember.

"At least you, señorita, you don't talk much. You don't make so much racket. You're like Laura."

"Who is Laura?"

Ah, yes, now she remembered about my girlfriend. I had already told her about it. She begged my pardon. Then immediately she began to forget again.

"Drive down this street. Now take this one. Now I'm going to die." Everything was just that easy.

After a while she too began to get bored with just driving around and she went back to the same subject.

"The custom of formal engagement is something that shouldn't be abandoned. But today all moral standards have gone to the dogs. Nowadays you see these young girls who…"

She went on about that for maybe half an hour or forty-five minutes. The only way I could keep from telling her to shut up was by putting Laura between my mind and my fly.

"We do everything in silence. We read each other's lips and we know what's happening," somehow came out of my mouth.

Oops, I shouldn't have said that. She loved those kinds of relationships where couples can understand each other with "just a single look." But that's not what I said… I said "the lips." Looks still didn't tell me a thing.

"Well, I'm speaking metaphorically, like you"—*when did I ever talk like that, pendeja?*—"It must be very nice to have a romance that is so romantic."

"I don't think it has anything to do with that, señorita. Like I told you, I taught Laura to read lips."

She opened her mouth. She still didn't understand.

"I…taught…her…to read…lips."

She didn't believe me then, but by the time we had gone up Reforma on our way to the Centro, she knew the whole story: my mother, may God rest her soul, was deaf, poor thing. Everyone in my house had to learn to read lips so then we could teach Ma. I remember we all talked like that. It was a family of silences. That must be why I can't stand a lot of racket.

Once again I had caught myself remembering and again it was because of her. Not even the places I passed by in the taxi used to set off my memory, and that woman had found out how to wipe away my forgetfulness.

"So," she replied, "I'd better be very careful about whispering my thoughts, even though you know it's very rude to listen in on other people's intimate secrets."

Maybe so, but it was fun.

At last we were quiet for a good while. I even thought then about my mamacita's deafness. I was about eight years old when she lost her hearing, so I could compare how she'd been before and after. Before she was like any other mom, shouting, sad, worried. But afterwards, when she was deaf, she became soft; it was because she was cut off from the good and the bad, both the hassles and the hopes. She became pure like a wild animal; her love for us was the only thing that kept her going. It looks to me like the whole world spits its truths into our ears, and now the truth is so many truths that you wind up never knowing what the truth is. Words must be the instrument the Devil uses to lead people astray, the way I see it.

In that moment the old lady was saying something about advances in communication or some such garbage. Me, I wasn't even paying attention.

7

A One-Star Hotel

WE WENT TO A HOTEL near the Centro, in a grayish business district between the tourist area and an area that was a disaster zone even without an earthquake. It was like lukewarm water: a neighborhood that had fallen unconscious, driven into the cement by the weight of time, colorless, a neighborhood I didn't know. As I got out of the car I saw the two old men turning the corner arm in arm.

"Something happened to me in this hotel many years ago," she said in a deep, mysterious voice.

I thought there was no way she was a virgin, but I kept my mouth shut. (She never told me what it was that had happened to her there. She didn't tell me all her secrets.)

I went into the hotel with the packages from the car as she was heading toward the stairs with the keys. I walked behind her. On the first step she turns around and bumps into me. Like nothing had happened, I swerved a little and kept going on up the stairs.

"Where do you think you're going? Wait for me. Here, take the key to your room. It's across the hall from mine."

We both opened the doors to our rooms, but before she went into hers she said, "Give me my toiletries bag. Oh, and it wouldn't be a bad idea to wash the car."

"Right now?"

The words bounced against the door.

From in front of the black Ford I saw how the light came on in Barbara's room, so she could keep an eye on me. Her figure in silhouette looked pretty, in spite of her sixty years. I shook out the floor mats and cleaned the black curves of the car until they looked like mirrors; its dark shape was shining. After all, the car had a woman's body. That's how all the girls must have looked in the old lady's day. It had an enormous humped back and round headlights covered with chrome. Made of strong metal. An old-fashioned design with a rounded hood and a windshield split in two. Leather seats and an incredibly fancy radio.

In the polished metal I saw the light in her room go out. I leaned against the car to smoke a cigarette and waited until it was all gone. Then I went to my room and closed the door.

She couldn't sleep. She tried more positions than there are for screwing, but she couldn't relax. Then she got up from the bed and went to look out the window. That's when she saw a Ford (just like her own) pulling up in front of the hotel. A chauffeur from the thirties got out of the car to open the doors. Then Barbara's mother got out of one side of the car and her father got out of the other, and then finally she herself got out, but she was nine years old. They all went into the hotel and the grown-up Barbara followed them with her gaze.

She waited, sitting on her bed. Everything was dimly lit and along the edge of the door a line of light entered the room. There were footsteps of people climbing the stairs. She heard her own voice as a child: "Don't cry any more, Mamacita. If you'd like, I'll give you a kiss."

Memories swirled around outside her. Barbara opened the door, hoping to see her mother. The decor changed completely and now she was in her house. (It was a house from the days of don Porfirio, like that other passenger had told me about.) Still, she didn't see her mother or herself as a nine-year-old but just a pair of doors that closed at the same time. She went to her parents' bedroom and she listened before she went in:

"Tía Mercedes told me they couldn't board the ship. That she didn't even see them on the pier. My God! There were even some people who shot themselves right there—can you imagine?—at the edge of the sea."

"We'll have word about them soon," said the voice of her father, without a Spanish accent. "Don't let it worry you, dear."

"But they're my parents! I haven't seen them since you brought me to Mexico, before the war."

Barbara's anxiety drove the ghosts away when she opened the door to embrace her parents. Instead of finding them, she bumped into me. She was deflated. For an instant her eyes were like smoked glass that didn't reflect anyone.

"What's wrong?"

"What?… Nothing, nothing," she said nervously.

I was going to turn the light on, but she didn't want me to. She closed the door little by little and went off to her own room. She sat down in front of the window and she fell asleep like that, watching the black car.

THE NEXT DAY I woke up first. That dumb-ass uniform again. The whole thing was fucking with my mind. I was grey and the uniform a little bit greyer. I may have even become invisible. It was just a matter of putting up with the old bitch a little while longer, taking her money and stealing the car. And if I felt sorry for her, so what. That's life.

That night I had a dream:

I was standing in front of the Ford. Barbara was watching me from the hotel window. I got into the car, and with my lips only I told her adiós, and she understood. I took off and tromped on the gas pedal. I think I wanted to kill myself, but I didn't know why. The thing is—well, at least as far as I remember—it's that all the traffic lights turned green, and I was waiting for a red light, or even a yellow light, to pull out a pistol and kill myself, but they were all green and let me keep going; when one was just about to turn red, I'd get to the corner, driving along like that, and *boom* the light would turn green. And me driving and driving and driving. And I was getting tired, within the tired feeling of the dream, and I wanted to stop so bad it hurt, but I had no choice but to keep going. Just like that until finally I got out of the city, alive.

Before I knocked on Barbara's door I was going over the dream in my mind so I could tell her about it. But for some reason I can't remember I never got around to telling her.

Knock, knock. Finally she answered, with the sheet still covering her clear up to her nose. And so once again I had to wait for her.

Then we went down to the hotel restaurant, and there were other people besides us.

We ate breakfast without speaking. Small talk at that hour drives me up the wall. I was sitting at a separate table, next to hers, like the time she gave me the uniform. She really took her role seriously, and it just wasn't that big a deal. When we were drinking our coffee...

"This hotel used to be a first-class one, and now it's eighth class." She made me take a look around at the people in the place. "Of course these aren't the sort of people who used to come here in my day."

And why should that matter to me? She was the one who had chosen it, right?

"Maybe I was mistaken; at night all cats look black... But no, this is the hotel I was looking for. What a shame! How things change as time goes by!"

I looked her up and down, to show her how right she was. She didn't even notice.

"I'm sure you understand perfectly what I'm talking about…" *Me? No way.* "I mean this hotel could be one of the ones they call 'one night hotels.' You must know about them, or don't you?"

Now what? Was she trying to suggest something by any chance?

"What's going on? Is this how it's going to be between us now?"

"By no means. That's why you're sitting at your table and I'm sitting at mine."

Then she explained. "When I asked you that, it was not with any improper intention, as you think, but because you do have the bad habit of 'reading' other people's conversations."

"Well, you're wrong. As a matter of fact, I'm not even doing it right now."

She didn't believe me. She said she saw me doing it, but I swear I wasn't; I was just looking at my eggs and frijoles, and that's all. But she wouldn't let up, saying who knows what I had already learned about the couples that were eating breakfast, and one thing and another. Jesus!

"But when?" I protested.

"One has to be very careful around you. You've got morbid curiosity."

"Come on! You're even going to accuse me of that?"

She ate her eggs and I ate mine angrily. Two or three bites went by slowly, and then she started in again, "Actually, I don't think it's really true that you can read lips."

I didn't say a word. I didn't take the trouble to answer her.

"That's another bad habit you have."

The same, my mouth was glued shut.

"You're a liar," she said at last.

The old lady wanted to force me to say something, to prove to her that I did know how to read lips. But no way. Let her keep right on wanting.

"Let's see. What are those ones over there saying?"

"It looks to me like you're the one who wants to know what everyone's saying." I couldn't take it anymore, and I threw the words in her face.

"You're crazy! What I like to do is expose mythomaniacs like you."

"Mytho-what's?"

I was tired of all this. Then I starting doing things her way.

"Okay, if you're so sure I'm a liar, that's fine. What have I got to lose by telling you what you want to hear?"

She got furious. "You're…you're…despicable!"

She started eating her food in huge bites. I could hardly keep from laughing. But then she stopped eating and looked sadly at the rest of her food. I felt sorry for her. That's why I started doing what I'm even better at than driving: reading other people's lips.

I looked at the couple of lovers and started: "What are we going to tell your brother?"

Barbara caught on right away; she raised her head and her eyes lit up.

I went on with the girl's answer, even imitating her voice: "I don't care whether Chucho likes you or not. Besides, he's only my half-brother. So we don't have to tell him anything. I'm a grown woman and I can do whatever I feel like without having to explain my actions to anyone. I came here because I wanted to, not because anyone made me. You know perfectly well I can't live with my family anymore. I want to be who I am, an independent woman. So the best thing is for us to start looking for a place to live together, right?"

Barbara raised her eyebrows and shook her head, but even so she couldn't hide how much she was enjoying this little game.

"Go on," she told me.

Now I imitated the boy's voice. He coughed nervously at hearing such a proposition.

"Well, all I'm waiting for is to get the yes and I'll do it."

And now the girl spoke: "But I've already said yes a thousand times."

"I'm talking about my old lady saying yes about giving me a divorce."

Barbara lowered her head to hide her laughter. Then she looked up very seriously when I imitated the girl's anger: "What? You jerk…! You rotten…!"

"Okay, okay. That's enough. I believe you." Barbara interrupted me a little impatiently.

When I finished my breakfast I held in my usual burp because now I was in the company of a lady, although Laura also got mad when I did it in front of her. I went outside to do it. Barbara paid and when she came outside she told me to wait there a little while. As she crossed the street to go into one of those dusty old book stores, I started warming up the car.

She was old, and the car was too, and the street was even older, the hotel, the book store, the whole district. Blaaah!

I don't know what you call what's wrong with me, but sometimes I get this nausea that isn't in my belly, but from some wrinkle or other in my body. I get sick, I feel like I want to puke when I'm around people. And suddenly I felt like I couldn't take another second around that old woman who bugged me so much, who made me want to slap the shit out of her. I felt again the urgent need to get out of there. The pisser is that, as usual, I don't know where to go, because in any other place and with any other person the same thing would happen to me. It even used to happen with Laura sometimes. I retched inside, and I calmed myself by imagining how I'd take the old bitch for all her money, that I'd take her Ford and I'd leave Mexico City at last, for some other place, because there had to be some other place, no matter how far away it was, goddamn it. Don't tell me there isn't some little corner of this lousy world where I can feel good. What a fucking rotten deal if there isn't.

But then I didn't think any more because she was coming toward the car carrying a book called *Manual of Courtesy and Good Manners* by a guy named Carreño. Or something like that.

8

First Paycheck

IN THE CAR AGAIN, bound for who knows where, but with the tank full and '40s music playing, we slowly headed away from the downtown area. The music was always the same on identical stations: World Radio, Radio 6.20 and all those ones from the old days, you know? As I was making a turn at twenty kilometers an hour to get onto Reforma by the side of the Lotería, I took a chance and said what was on my mind.

"I don't want to bother you, señora…señorita. But I'd like to know how often you're going to pay me…you understand…"

"I don't know. How often do you wish to be paid?"

"Well, look. Things are really messed up and every day it gets worse. I mean, money isn't worth a thing any more, you see?"

She was lost in contemplation of the street, looking at everything: houses, people, sidewalks, walls, shop windows. It was like she wasn't paying any attention to me, so I shifted to first at forty kilometers an hour so the jolt would wake her up.

"You tell me what you want."

"How about every weekend, does that seem okay to you? So I've got something to work with."

Once again she turned to the street. But anyway she said that it was fine. This time I shifted into third at twenty kilometers an hour, to lug the engine. I asked her to give me something in advance, and she said it was no problem. After I heard that, I shifted into first, second and third just the way it was meant to be done.

When I was about to say something—now I can't even remember what it was—she took the money from her purse and I almost started to drool. I was watching it all through the rear view mirror which I adjusted to follow her movements. Then Barbara realized that I was watching her and shifted around trying to get out of range of the mirror. For a minute I lost sight of her. I panicked and turned to look at her directly, and at that moment she came out of who-knows-where to lean against the back of my seat.

"Take this."

She gave me the book. Her jokes were never any good, and this was one of the worst. I had to play along with her if I wanted to get paid. So I laughed. I said I'd read it when I got a chance, and she replied that it was the best thing I could do if I wanted to improve my manners. She said something or other like that I was very crude.

I opened the book and found my pay. Stuck in the 8 A.M. traffic of bureaucrats, I could read the paragraphs the crazy old woman had underlined for me without neglecting my driving: *The individual who generally does nothing but listen to others demonstrates an unsociable personality, or, perhaps, an absolute lack of intellectual wherewithal, both of which circumstances exclude him from all circles of cultivated and well-mannered people.*

"But it doesn't say here that it's bad to read other people's lips."

"It's the same thing," she answered in an obnoxious tone.

I skimmed through other paragraphs while a stupid traffic police-man screwed up the traffic even more than before and in addition got totally pissed off at a stoplight that wouldn't obey his orders. *Courtesy*—I continued reading—*demands that we appear to take an*

unqualified interest in the conversation of others, even when we do not
feel naturally moved to do so.

"I'd say, in fact, that this is more about you, since you don't pay any attention to anyone, you're just all wrapped up in your own little world."

"What?"

"Oh, nothing."

I went on driving. Another street and another and another. Slowly, as if time was the private property of the three of us (with the Ford as a partner, of course).

Nowadays there were almost no apartments in the Centro. Just offices. Some were very run down: torn curtains, dirty windows, I could almost smell the dust, the filth.

"Before, they used to look so splendid here in this area. The lawyer Chavarría had his office on Donceles. It was so elegant! I can remember that his secretary, Miss María Cárdenas, would wear shoulder pads much higher than we used to wear in that era. Ah, and she never went out on the street without a hat, even though people were already starting to neglect that item which proper women should never have stopped wearing."

It smelled of rotten wood. No doubt there were still typewriters there as old as the hills. Suddenly I felt like a prisoner. A few more streets, more like a prisoner. I hated the old lady more than ever. I pulled up to the curb right beside a No Parking sign. I turned around to look at her and at that moment I remembered the roll of bills—*so hang in there, guy, just a little while longer*—and I softened the look on my face to say to her, "Why don't I teach you to read lips? It's really cool…"

"What?"

"The thing is that I get tired of driving and driving all around and then with this fucking tra…"

Her eyes shut my mouth up. They almost popped out of her head from sheer outrage. I turned red! Really, red with shame. What the hell was going on? What did this old woman have that gave her such power over me time after time? What could she have? To tell you the truth, I couldn't see that she had anything at all.

"Juan, I'm going to ask you, please, that in front of me you behave correctly. You must understand that I'm a lady and that these vulgarities are offensive to me. I think you can do it. Stop swearing! Do you understand?"

I turned back to the wheel, now purple with rage. I was thinking that it was just going to be for a short time, for sure, because if she didn't die soon, I would end up killing her with my very own hands.

9

The Cine Parisiana

IT WAS ABOUT 9:30 in the morning the next day when we were
driving down Reforma going nowhere, with the radio tuned to that
damned station with music from silent films. The sun was beginning
to beat down on us, which is why my left arm is a lot darker than my
right one. I hadn't put up with that burning sun on my elbow for
seven years for nothing. And on top of that I was tired. The Ford
didn't have air conditioning and my head was throbbing from all the
noise. The glare from the black hood made me see visions of I-don't-
know-what.

Damn! Back when I was driving the taxi I'd just be enjoying a
leisurely breakfast at this hour. And now, on the other hand!

I had to rob the bitch. Fate had put her in my life so that I could
change my luck. I knew it, but that's as far as it went, because I
couldn't do anything to her. I started imagining things; you get so
you can drive without having to use your head at all; the hands and
the feet learn how to move by themselves.

She was coming down the stairs of a hotel. It was a very strange
hotel because I've never seen one like it around here. The stairs led
right out onto the street. Ah, now that I think about it, I once saw a
house like that on a gringo television show, but it wasn't a hotel; it

was an apartment house that was just like all the others on the street. Well, it doesn't matter anyway, it was a hotel and Barbara was coming down the stairs fast and watching the steps so that she wouldn't fall and carrying in her hand a big box of something or other that was shining like it was gold. She was wearing a fur coat. I was watching her from the sidewalk across the street, leaning against the car. She came running across the street, and her scarf (because she was wearing a scarf over her hair) was floating in the air. She didn't look bad at all. Past her prime, sort of old, but pretty, attractive; she reminded me of a movie actress of her day, but I don't know who because to tell you the truth I hadn't seen more than one or two of those old films. So she got to the car and I opened the door for her.

Once we were under way she ordered me to take her to the Cine Parisiana in the Juárez district. I told her no way, that there was no Cine Parisiana there. And like a stubborn fool she kept saying there was. So fine, I took her there, without moving my eyes for a second from the golden box I could see in the rear view mirror.

When we got there I turned around to look at her and looked smack into her enormous smile, like it was a close-up, as they say, filling the whole screen. Winking one eye at me, she made me look out at the street. Yeah, there was the grand Cine Parisiana with its marquee all lit up, even though it wasn't nighttime but only afternoon. Ladies and gentlemen wearing hats and some bratty kids dressed like sailors.

"And why did you want to go to a movie with that box, señorita?"

"The manager of this theater is an uncle of mine and it has the best safe in Mexico, because they brought it directly from Washington. It's the only place where my money and jewelry will be safe."

We got out and she bought two tickets for the movie.

The show had already started.

"What time are you going to see your uncle?"

"I just want to see what the movie's about."

It was one with Bette Davis and George Brent, who was playing the part of a doctor. Bette Davis was rich and a total bitch. When she finds out she's going to die, she turns all nice and he marries her and they live happily for two weeks and then she dies and everyone cries forever.

Barbara let me sit beside her. I sensed her dry skin—well, it really wasn't all that dry—beneath the red fur of her coat. It must have been made of that mink they're always talking about on the TV.

She watched and watched the film. She cried and cried. I started getting impatient because I couldn't get up my nerve and so I didn't take advantage of that perfect moment to grab her box and run off in the darkness, jump in the Ford and—adiós, see you around. I think I even tensed all my muscles to build up my courage.

When Bette Davis is good and sick, I make a lunge and *bam!* I grab the box she has sitting on her legs and start to run up the dark aisle. Barbara didn't cry out, absolutely nothing happened. What could be going on? I went out onto the street carrying the box, but I couldn't see the car. Damn! I had been so nervous about robbing her that I didn't notice where I had parked it.

I looked all around. There was no sign of the car. Behind me, inside the theater, it seemed like there was a major uproar getting under way: shouts, whistles, people running around.

I ran too and turned the corner. The Ford wasn't there either. I ran around another corner. Nothing. And then a third corner. Nothing. I ran the whole way around the block: mysteriously the Ford was parked in front of the Cine Parisiana as if it were impossible for it to have gone somewhere else all by itself.

By this time all the people had come out of the theater. In her big fur coat Barbara was there in front of the crowd on the sidewalk. I crouched and ran along the opposite sidewalk hoping no one would see me. I opened the door and got into the car.

I was about to take off when temptation overcame common sense: I picked up the box and was about to open it when...

"Son of a bitch! Another red light."

"Juan, restrain yourself!"

The goddamn red light had broken the thread of my fantasy. Now I'd never know what was in the box.

It was just then that a boy who couldn't have been more than sixteen years old—passing himself off as a street vendor, because he was among a group of them—came over to the car as I was trying to get back into my fantasy, and with a jerk ripped off my wrist watch, leaving me with nothing but a white tattoo on my wrist.

"Motherfucker!" And I jumped out of the car.

"What's going on, Juan?" the old bitch said like an idiot.

I took off running down the street, but all the vendors were in cahoots and they kept cutting me off as I ran through the cars. I saw him disappear with my quartz watch among the newsboys shouting of *Excélsior* and *Novedades*.

I came back empty-handed.

"But what was that all about, Juan. Are you all right?"

"I've been robbed, that's what it's all about."

"How horrible! And how is it that I didn't even know? No, these days there's just no way to live a decent life in this city. What a..."

Okay, okay. I plugged my ears so I couldn't hear the old lady run on. Really, old people are horrible, it seems to me. All I knew was that the son of a bitch had run off with part of my salary in the shape of a watch. I could see that the dumb bitch's mouth kept talking, but I didn't feel like deciphering any of it.

What I realized, though, was that Barbara was concerned about me. I think it was at that moment that I started to learn something about eyes.

"It happened so fast. Suddenly you… Oh, my Lord! A robbery at this hour of the day… Was your watch a good one?"

"It was expensive." And just then I got a brilliant idea. "Really expensive, believe me, and here I am with no money."

Everything turned out just the way I thought it would. She sat there quietly, without moving her lips. The old lady intrigued me, because I didn't know what she was going to do. Then she told me to pull the car into the parking lot near the *Excélsior* building. I knew she was hiding something in her wrinkles, and so I jumped out in a hurry to open the door for her. The parking lot attendants stood there watching her. It wasn't very often that a chauffeur pulled into one of those parking lots, with his *patrona* and all, but what the hell. She got out and walked away with her head held high. She had a funny way of walking, no, not funny, I'd say it was sort of saucy, with her head thrown back and everything from the waist down thrust forward. Anyway I followed her about three steps behind. She stopped in front of a store window and I wasn't paying attention and kept on walking. When I turned around she was already inside looking at skirts. I waited and finally she came out with no packages; she was just acting like she could afford to buy something.

We walked on. She looked like a young girl from some other time. If it weren't for the years, I guess she'd be a young girl. Every once in a while someone going the other way started watching her from the corner of Robert's and ended up smiling all the way to the Cine París. Then I thought I must look as ridiculous as she did and decided to walk four steps behind her. Another old lady, but one a lot older than Barbara, also came by going the other way. She looked at Barbara, smiled, and nodded her head like she was greeting her. Just to be safe I dropped back another step; now I was five steps behind. Then I lost another one because a gringa with a great ass passed by. We got close to Insurgentes and stopped at that place where they say Buendía was killed.

"I don't have much time. When you see a watch shop, tell me."

"But we already passed a ton of them."

"A ton of what?"

"Of watch shops."

"Why do you say a ton?"

"Oh, for God's sake, forget it. I just mean we passed a lot of watch shops. I even told you so."

"Excuse me. I wasn't…"

"Well, anyhow. I already told you."

"When did you tell me?"

"A little while ago, when we passed one."

"I don't remember. Anyway, you'll tell me when we get to the next one, right?"

That old woman never gave up.

Finally we went into a jewelry store and came out in a little while with a new watch and with empty stomachs. So we ended up eating breakfast at Shirley's. I came out ahead: the watch she bought me was worth five times as much as my old quartz one.

10

Everything the Same, But Different

SHE LOVED GOSSIP, as much as she claimed she didn't. She was the nosiest person in the world—I mean, it's not so unusual to be that way, that is, for men; but old women are really terrible, I swear.

One day, eating in a little restaurant in the Roma district—she at her table and me at another—she wanted me to translate for her a conversation between a pair of old folks. What I did gave her pleasure. I even did the voices of the old man and the old woman and she liked that—what I mean is that it made her happy and I felt good. I exaggerated the gestures and the voices. She was laughing. Now I can see her again in my memory as if I was seeing her from far away, behind the windows of a restaurant lost in the past...

Well, the talk those folks were having was, to tell you the truth, more boring than an educational TV channel. The longer I went on with the game, the sleepier it made me.

"That's enough, no?" I said at last.

"Why don't you want to do it any more?"

"Because it's not funny."

"They've been together all their lives."

"That's the problem. They don't have any thing more to say to each other."

"And that's not funny, right?"

"Right."

"I wonder what they said when they were falling in love with each other?"

"Just what everyone always says at those times."

"So everything in life is just one long repetition?"

"Well, yeah, no?… I don't know, I never think about things like that."

"Yes, everything repeats itself but it's also always different. Ay, Juan, we have no defenses. No protection from anything."

Híjole, she had a way of saying things like that: that's the way it is, there you have it, you can do whatever you damn well please with it. This business of us not having any defenses really got to me. I didn't understand it, to tell you the truth, but it really got to me.

She finished eating first and turned to look at the couple again. She said again that she'd never been married and that maybe that was the best thing that could have happened to her. That it was better to be alone than to be with someone, because that way it was twice as tedious.

"Oh, sure," I threw out at her. "You got all the answers, don't you? Why are you so negative, anyway?"

"I'm not negative, Juan. Or I don't know, maybe that's what happens to you when you see how life is. At any rate it's a good way to spare yourself a lot of frustration."

"Like what happened to that fox that said something or other was no good just because she couldn't eat it herself."

She got really pissed off again. She half closed her eyes and her lips got so tight they disappeared.

"Are you through eating?" she asked me, furious.

Boy, what a change in personality!

"As a matter of fact, no. I eat slowly. Why?"

She didn't answer me. And damned if she didn't grab my plate from under my nose and give it to a waiter who was passing by.

"What are you going to do?"

Again she didn't answer. She looked at my watch and right away I covered it with my hand so she couldn't take it from me. I realized that the mean old bitch was even meaner than I was.

"Bring me the check!" she shouted.

I calmed down for my own good. I lowered my eyes like I was about to get to my knees, but in a minute I looked back up with an idea.

"Why don't you let me teach you how to read lips? That way you wouldn't be pestering me and you might even have a good time."

She didn't say anything to me, she just turned to look at a table where two girls and a guy were sitting.

"It's not hard. And anyway, we've got plenty of time to spare."

"I don't have much."

"Well, whatever you've got, no?"

We looked at each other real serious. We were so solemn that we broke out laughing, like death was laughing as it chased after the old Ford. Suddenly I felt...great. I thought about how when I was with that damn Laura we only laughed when we were drunk, hollow bursts of laughter empty at the core. In the end, they hurt.

Then she nodded softly: she was giving me the chance to teach her the secret language of the lips. And I sat down at her table.

11

Resignation

THAT NIGHT it was hotter than a bitch. Barbara was alone in her hotel room with the windows open and the hot wind was fluttering her robe of fine cloth (she said it was made of moiré). She looked at herself in the mirror, reminiscing as usual, and her hand, as if it were a man's hand, caressed her face. She did it to her lips too. With her mouth she silently formed the letters *A, E, I, O, U* and she felt them with her fingertips, practicing the first lesson.

She got bored and went to the window. She saw me leaning against the Ford finishing a cigarette. I saw her as I took the last drag from the butt. I acted like I hadn't seen her and went to a telephone booth. I dialed a number and she stayed there in the window, hidden in the shadows of the room. Actually, I didn't see her, but I knew she was there. Laura answered the phone and among other things I had to explain to her that I hadn't seen her because a business deal was eating up all my time. I told her I missed her and that I thought about her a lot when I was in bed. She ended up hornier than I was. I promised I'd see her soon. She suspected that it had something to do with the car, but I didn't tell her what.

"You're not working as a chauffeur, are you?"

"No, of course not."

"That would be the last thing we need."

I didn't say anything. So now she wasn't only reading lips, she was reading minds too, goddamn woman.

"Hello?… Juan?… Are you there?"

"I have to go. I'll see you soon. I'll let you know when."

After I hung up I realized that Barbara was no longer at the window.

Lying back in her bed she closed her eyes. The telephone rang in the room next door. A voice which she recognized as her mother's voice answered, sobbing: "It's not possible. My God, it's not possible. Are you certain, Tía?

Barbara opened her eyes and listened more closely.

She heard her father's steady voice trying to calm his wife, but with little success. Her mother kept talking, almost to herself: "They can't find my parents. Everything is lost. I tell you it's all finished." "You'll wake up the child," he said. Barbara was wide awake now, but she began to fall asleep again. Little by little she moved away from the voices which grew more and more faint. Good night…

The next morning I woke up feeling refreshed, like I was happy to be alive. I woke her up as usual, because I was hungry. She answered politely, but coldly. Her nightmares had helped to put her in a sour mood. She came out of her room more quickly than usual and right away we went to get breakfast.

"It's nine o'clock sharp," I said, looking at my new wrist watch. "Okay. And what's on the agenda for today?" I asked her like you'd ask a tour guide.

"The same," she answered even more coldly as she sat down at her own table. I didn't know if I should do the same thing or sit with her. "Whatever," I said to myself, and reached for a chair, but she grabbed my hand, holding it fast. She didn't look me in the eyes, she just stared at my hand. She did it in such a strange way that even I looked down at my own hand, as if she were the one who had put it there and not me. I put the chair back in its place and sat down at the next table.

I was going to ask her something, but Barbara made a face, a scowl, which meant I wasn't supposed to say anything for maybe ten or fifteen minutes. We just ate.

Finally I said, "Why don't we go somewhere outside the city?"

"No, we'll keep on driving around my streets."

"What's so special about your streets?" I said it softly, but I was pissed, because you wake up feeling good about life and then, fuck!— the hopeless old bitch blows it all to hell. If you only knew how much I love the open road. I feel…you know, real light, my shoulders straight, not carrying the weight of this city on my back.

"We're not leaving the city."

"But every day it's from the Ribera district to the Roma to the Hipódromo and to the Centro and then the same-old same-old from one to the other to the other until…"

I might as well go on eating; she wasn't there anyway. For an instant I imagined that Barbara's whole being climbed into her own eyes and that her eyes took flight and carried her off to a place so far away that only old people or hermits could know of it.

Then I wanted to think about it some more, but the thought wouldn't come.

The truth was that she wasn't the least bit interested in anything about me. But that was fine, right? She had hired me to drive and that was it. The most important thing was her, because she was going to die, that was all that mattered.

While Barbara was eating here and her mind was traveling out there I looked her over, from head to toe, inch by inch, dwelling on a mole, a little brownish splotch, a dark glimmer in her skin. What could she be dying from? She would never tell me. Her eyes didn't look yellow, they weren't protruding, they didn't have a milky dead look anywhere or pupils like a cat, they weren't crossed or anything.

Then her neck: the big vein pulsed without hesitation, normally, beneath her white skin. Her breasts weren't bad at all. Without realizing it, I was beginning to get turned on by the analysis. You could still wrap your arm around her waist; and her legs were young looking, as if they had forgotten to get old along with the rest of her body. I went back to the top again and looked at her blonde hair: strange, dyed, because by sixty years old everything has lost its color. She had spots, like any old woman, but on her they looked like freckles. Her skin was cracked, but it was like the skin of those elegant white dolls. She knew how to fix herself up and nostalgia helped her know how to dress. Old women have something the young ones just don't have. I was beginning to know her: to understand that no one could ever really know her. For a brief moment I didn't want to bother her. I even felt sorry that she was going to die.

"How about going on with the lessons?" I said just to start a conversation. The important thing was the tone I used when I said it—friendly, so that she'd catch on that I felt okay with her, there, in the restaurant.

She just moved her head slightly and I think she said it was all right.

"Let's see. Tell me what I'm saying."

I moved my lips very slowly. She looked at me, and then lowered her eyes, and then I felt her gaze move to my mouth again. I said the word to her again clearly.

"No. Not yet. It's too soon."

"Try it; I'm just saying single words."

The waitress came to take our order and distracted her from my lips. When she left with the order Barbara looked at my mouth, waiting for me to say something. I intentionally didn't do anything. But then I played along…because I didn't want to annoy her that day, you know.

"Ma…má."

I said another word with just my lips.

"Den."

"No, look closely, silly."

"Dead."

"Oh, darn it. One more time."

"Dad."

"That's it! Very good."

The rest of the people in the restaurant caught on to our little game. I sat down at her table like I was courting her.

"We should continue later," she said. "People are noticing."

"No. Now it's my turn."

She didn't say anything to me and I chose two guys who were way at the back of the place, next to the big jar of chicharrones. I started:

"I'm sick and tired of my job, Juan." ("He's got the same name as me," I said). "I swear I can't take it any longer."

Then the friend said, "Are you going to get depressed again?"

"I've got a good reason; if you only knew how boring it is. I do absolutely nothing in the office—and that's about what they pay me as well."

"I wouldn't exactly say I'm lying on a bed of roses, but I'm not as negative as you are."

"Because you're so...I don't know. I swear that if it weren't for paydays and the few moments we have together..."

I got all tongue-tied, and Barbara started choking: two queers! I went on with a whiney little voice:

"Juan, really."

"And how do you think I feel?"

"No more," the old lady interrupted.

"Why not? It's just starting to get fun."

"No! That's perverted, and listening to it is even more perverted."

"You're talking crazy."

"I said that's enough," the old lady said curtly. "Read what I say to you instead."

Then she moved her mouth. When I read her lips I was pissed as hell. She noticed it, because she said, "What? Did I say something wrong? Or didn't you understand? I'll repeat it, but watch closely, okay?"

Again she said without a sound, "Take me to the bank to deposit the money I've been carrying around all over the place."

"Yeah, I understood, damn it." The *damn it* was to myself.

"So then let's go. I don't want it to get too late."

We left that place for the other one. I waited in the car while the greedy old bitch left her loot in safe keeping. It really bugged me. I promised myself never to wake up happy again. *And now how should I treat her?* I thought. I felt like quitting and skipping out with the Ford and everything. I could do it. The money was out of reach. I started the motor and the car rocked from one side to the other. It didn't run very well because I 'd spent all the money for repairs with Laura. So what? I shifted into first, but when I was letting out the clutch pedal, Barbara climbed into the back seat. Jesus! What timing! I pulled the car out, taking her with me. It must be God's will. That's how blind fate acts, without asking you whether you want it or not. It was obvious that there was no way for me to get rid of her.

"It's all done. Let's go," the dead woman said, as if nothing had happened.

12

Holding Tight to the Steering Wheel

GOING ALONG SAN COSME, an avenue full of candy vendors and contraband, it occurred to her to say that what she had put in the bank hadn't been much, just what she had made from the sale of old furniture and some old dresses that she didn't wear any more. *Something is better than nothing*, I told myself silently. She also said that she didn't want to go around carrying money with her everywhere. "It's dangerous to go out on the streets these days…"

"Opportunity makes the thief. Isn't that so, Juan?"

It was all right: I couldn't steal the money from her, but I could steal the car, and that was going to hurt her more. I got an image, and laughed while I was picturing it, of the old lady riding up and down the streets of her youth in a communal taxi, and then one day she would take one of those Route 100 buses all the way from the train station to the University and there she'd kick the bucket, with her eyes open. But before then… And what if the money runs out before I make off with the car? *Then what?* I thought.

"Señorita, what if you run out of money before you…before you…?"

She didn't answer me because her gaze was wandering aimlessly along the facades of houses.

"Slow down," she ordered me, and I did it though I don't know why. "Slowly, more slowly."

I asked her what was going on, but she was still lost in some other world. Again she ordered me to go around the block. I couldn't because it was a one-way street going the other direction. She insisted. Well, all right, I did it. There aren't many houses any more on San Cosme and those that are there shouldn't be. I think that Barbara rebuilt the city from her memory.

It was like her gaze was flying up above time. I saw her in the mirror. Her voice sounded strange.

"No, I don't want to come down," she was saying. "I'm scared."

"But what of?"

I parked the car. She got out or maybe they took her out. Who knows? She walked up to a metal door of what looked like it had once been a school. She was talking to herself. I couldn't stand all this crazy stuff. I felt something like anxiety or maybe helplessness, it was horrible, I swear. Now I really wanted to get the hell out of there. Who the fuck was she talking to? The candy sellers and the smugglers were laughing at her. She didn't even notice. She ran back to the car. Super loca, no doubt about it. Barbara was nuts, I'll be goddamned if she wasn't.

"Let's go!"

"But…"

"Let's go! Quick!"

I didn't see anyone but I could have sworn that it was true, that someone was following her.

The damn bitch had passed her fear on to me. I put the car in first and popped the clutch like a wild man, leaving a patch of rubber on the pavement. And there we were, going eighty along the streets of the Centro! We were really out of control.

Like one of those guys who write stories, she was silently describing everything she was seeing in her sick mind. By reading her lips I learned that her Spanish mother was poking her head through the window to say to her, "My treasure, get out of the car, we're here now."

Then the father appeared.

"Come on, little one, we don't have your time."

"Don't talk to her like that," said the mother, "You'll frighten her."

"It's getting late and you know how strict they are in the Institute."

So, obviously, it was a school. Her imagination had taken her that far. So that's why she said, "I don't want to get out. I'm scared."

"Good girls always obey their mothers. You're going to have a good time here with other girls your age. They'll all be your friends. They're going to teach you how to behave like a señorita, you'll see. Everyone will like you and you want people to like you, don't you, cutey?"

"Yes," she said.

"Come on, sweetie, come with Mommy. I'm going to stay here with you on your first day of school."

Then her voice got gruff and shaky. "Keep going, keep going, don't stop any more until I tell you to!"

WE LEFT THOSE STREETS and said nothing more. I changed the rear view mirror to reflect my mouth so that I couldn't see hers or know any more about her pathetic existence. I read my own lips, and my secrets bounced around back and forth in a sort of a circle between me and me, with no real direction—they were just like the Ford and my mouth in the mirror.

I don't know how or why but I wound up behind the American Embassy. It was nighttime. Nothing had happened the whole damn afternoon, at least not from my seat to the windshield—in the back seat, God knows! I stopped the car. I was really pissed off, bitter.

"What is wrong with you? Tell me right now what's your problem. I've had it up to here with you!"

"Once again I demand that you do not speak to me in that way, we are not equals."

Then I asked her again nicely and she took it the wrong way, like supposedly I was threatening her. I asked her again, trying to calm her down.

"What do you care? I pay you to drive, not to ask me questions. Mind your own business and leave me in peace!"

That was really the last straw. I'd had it up to the eyeballs with her. What the fuck was I doing there after all? I took off the cap and the jacket without getting out of the car. "You can keep all this," I said. I didn't care any more about the car or about anything. As far as I was concerned she could die right then and there. "Go to hell!" I shouted at her. Things had gotten serious and I knew she knew it, because in the mirror I could see her change, like she was jamming the gear shift from first into second. And then, of course, she did a number on me. It wasn't the first time and it wouldn't be the last. She just knew how to do it, I guess.

"No, wait! What are you doing?"

"I'm leaving."

"Juan, please, stay, I'll pay you twice as much!"

I acted like I was thinking about it, and then like I was leaving. Without reading her lips I knew what she was going to propose to me—who knows, maybe now I could even read minds like Laura could!

"The car will be yours. I promise you. When I die."

"Yeah, right!"

"I swear to you; and what I said about your salary is true too."

"But what if you don't keep your word on either of those two things and besides, what if you don't die?"

She searched nervously for the money in her big black old lady's purse.

"Look, here's an advance."

As I grabbed the cash I looked her in the eye: the fog had lifted from her gaze. Her pupils were big, shiny, like full of a super-bright liquid; it almost seemed like she'd been smoking dope by the kilo. Her voice got really terrific—strong and deep but totally a woman's.

"Now you see that I do keep my word. And as for your other question…"—she began to sound just like someone who is reciting something—"you know that neither I nor anybody else can bribe death. I don't know when it will come for me, but I can assure you that it will be soon. It has already finished off most of me. Why don't you believe that I'm going to die in a few days? Don't you see how Death is tugging at me? Don't you hear when it comes close to whisper in my ear? You can't read its lips because you're still going about on the other shore, where Death is transparent, like air and water. But sooner or later you will make the jump to this side. We are all condemned to death from the first breath of life…without knowing why. Eternally not knowing why… Come on, Juan, be patient with me as I am patient with Time."

I said nothing. I didn't even dare to look at her. I just trembled a little.

Slowly I put the money in my pocket. The jacket felt like it weighed a ton when I put it on, the cap too. I was moving about in slow motion. Then I grabbed the steering wheel fiercely and looked toward the horizon.

"Fine. And now? Where to?"

"Nowhere. I'm dizzy and I want to rest a little. Then you can take me to the hotel."

I was beginning to get comfortable in my seat when she ordered me to clean the car first.

I knew perfectly well that it wasn't out of any habit of cleanliness that she was prodding my ass, but just a way for her to say, "Okay, I've raised your salary, the car will be yours, I'm going to die, I asked you not to leave me, but right now I fart the loudest and you just shut up and do what I tell you."

I tucked my balls in my pocket, opened the glove compartment and took out a rag; it was still a little wet from the water that had leaked in during the last rain.

Once again I went to work polishing the curves and making the black blacker. I saw myself reflected in the body and looked at her through the window: we weren't a good match.

On the sidewalk, some young boys were moving around. I looked closer: they were male whores hooking up with a bunch of guys in cars. I took a better look and saw family men who get their kicks eating tube steak.

Suddenly, one of them—probably the representative of the respectable guys—pulled his car right up to mine and just about drove up my tail pipe. So I crouched down to hide and pretended to clean the headlight. And damned if those headlights didn't come on again all by themselves, blinding me with the flash! Groping along the black curves with my hands, I managed to reach my window. For just a second I caught a glimpse of the Bony Bitch in the back seat. I blinked and tears of sorrow soaked my face. When I finally saw black, and in the blackness the black dress that Barbara always wore—I mean, when I saw Barbara herself asleep—I got in and turned off the lights. I didn't make a sound.

The last fag of the night was disappearing before I closed my eyes. Then I forgot to open them and instead I fell asleep.

13

The Fat Guy
and the Skinny Guy

IN THE MORNING there wasn't so much as a single policeman to
bother us, even though the Ford might have been a car bomb parked
in front of the gringo embassy. Barbara woke up in a good mood; she
didn't seem to be bothered at all by the night we spent in the car.

She was hungry and didn't know whether she should go take a
bath first or eat breakfast. Of course she chose the bath.

She didn't want to go to the restaurant in the hotel so we went to a
Sanborn's. She sat at her table and I sat at the one beside it, as usual.
She ordered molletes while I went to the restroom without knowing
I would find a faggot there washing his privates after a night's work.
It's always that way. As a taxi driver I was familiar with the routine of
men's rooms: in the morning it's washing up; at midday no one goes
there; in the evening respectable people use them and at night
everybody's masturbating.

We finished our breakfast and Barbara took advantage of the fact
that I wasn't wearing my jacket or cap—that is, that I didn't look like
her chauffeur—to invite me to sit at her table.

"Let's see how well my lessons are coming along," she said and chose a couple of chicks who were sitting beside us.

Actually, I was feeling so stiff and twisted from the night spent in the Ford that I didn't feel like talking. But the old woman looked so silly as she imitated the chicks' voices that I started to enjoy it.

"What time did he say he would come?" I clearly heard one of them say.

And Barbara repeated, "What time did he say he would come?"

"At twelve o'clock," the other one answered.

And again Barbara repeated, "At twelve o'clock."

"He's already late," the first one was speaking again.

Barbara: "He's already late."

"It's always that way," the other one concluded.

She made me laugh when she said, "It's always that way."

"This doesn't count," I said.

"Why?" she asked smiling.

"You can hear what they're saying from here."

"That's not true."

"You cheater."

"Cheater." I called her a cheater and we looked each other in the eyes. Twenty seconds went by on my new watch and at the twenty-first she started laughing like we were accomplices in our first robbery.

"Okay, fine, you choose which ever ones you want and I'll do it," the cheater said, still laughing.

I spotted two norteños who were eating far away from us, next to the cash register. She took out a pair of glasses which I had never seen before, put them on and then squinted to focus her vision. She was so caught up in just making out the words that the old fool wasn't conscious of what the conversation was about.

"Don't turn and look, but there's an old lady in the back who wants to pick us up," the fat one said.

To make matters worse, Barbara was moving her lips to reproduce what they were saying.

Without trying to hide it, the skinnny norteño turned and looked right at her.

"Ah! What a crazy old woman! Well, go for it, show them what a norteño can do with a mummy from Mexico City."

"That's enough," I told her anxiously.

"Wait, I think I…"

"Señorita, the check, please."

"But I was just beginning to understand them."

"They understood too, don't worry about that."

The fat one, who had thick, greasy lips, blew her a kiss and at last Barbara caught on.

"Oh, my God. I think…"

"I think so too. Señorita, hurry up with the check!"

By the time the waitress got there we had already left, but first Barbara had figured up the bill and even left a good tip.

"That's how these Mexico City people are: all show and no go."

I can't remember now if the fat guy or the skinny guy said that.

14

You Have To Know Where the Devil Is Leading You

WHEN WE WERE CROSSING the San Rafael district, Barbara wasn't in the car anymore. To escape from the embarrassment caused by the norteños, she had retreated to a place that not even the rear view mirror could find.

I got bored being by myself all this time, so I took off on my own route towards the south. Barbara reappeared, flying back like a witch who'd wandered off course, as soon as we left the San Rafael, and she gave me strict orders never to drive out of "her" Mexico City.

The map of the city was now drawn to her liking; that is, as it had been in the forties. If you crossed the boundary marked by the viaduct for Cuahtémoc, you would find yourself out in the middle of nowhere. And beyond the Tlaxcoaque bridge, the city didn't exist either, as far as we were concerned. It seemed to me that the city was growing smaller day by day, like still one more mouth that was closing and eating us up little by little.

Suddenly we were driving down Cinco de Febrero. We couldn't

get into the Centro because there was so much traffic. Later we found out that it was because of a demonstration. She told me that in her time that kind of thing was very unusual. That everyone was very happy though they wouldn't realize it till later.

She had me leave the car in a parking lot around there, and she took me for a walk alongside Sanborn's House of Tiles—that is, behind the Post Office. She wanted to see the Centro, she said, because she hadn't seen it for a long time and because her father had told her that behind the Post Office was the street where the first traffic jam had occurred: one carriage was going one way and another was going in the opposite direction; neither one wanted to yield the right of way to the other and a viceroy had to solve the problem, because it was during the colonial period. The two gentlemen deigned to retreat (her words) at the same time. The whole mess lasted more than a week. She ended up saying that the city hadn't changed much since then.

She also asked me if I had seen the movie *In the Palm of Your Hand*, with Andrea Palma and Arturo de Córdova, so handsome. Of course I haven't seen it, I answered. It seems they shot some scenes two streets away from where we were walking. She had seen it all because she had rented them the Ford for the movie.

"Really?"

"Yes, my car appears in it."

"Why did you rent it to them?"

"That's how I made my living, can you believe it? I didn't have a husband to support me like all the other women had."

She seemed to remember something after she'd laughed a little.

"My last suitor was a minor politician of the time. And although no one came up to my father's level, my family was very enthusiastic about the boy. But after all that, you know what? All of them are dead now."

She barely whispered that, although I thought I could read something more on her lips.

We walked for a good while until she got tired. I went to get the car and I picked her up on 20 de Noviembre Avenue like at about seven o'clock at night. It didn't occur to me to leave her there and make off with the Ford, as I had planned. It wasn't until I saw her standing there waiting for me that I remembered. A lot of time would go by before I would figure that one out, like it also would before I understood why she always dressed in black.

She was going to get in her Ford right on a corner where the whores are the most miserable because what they get paid is next to nothing, like their lives—because there are so many of them, they rule the streets. She didn't tell me where we were going; she just stood there silently, looking at them.

"Aren't you going to get in?"

"Well! In my days they used to be out there by Vizcaínas, but now there are a lot of them everywhere you go. It's absolutely clear that the city has really changed."

"And not that it's exactly the same? You just said that a while ago."

"That's true too, Juan."

Then she held her head up high.

"It's disgusting. When I was young a respectable girl could go all over the city with no fear of these unpleasant encounters. But now there's no respect. We've all lost our place." She moved towards me and said very softly, "You know what? When I go out on the street, I have the feeling that someone is always waiting for me, to rape me."

What extremes! First she was like the Queen of Sheba; then she was a little girl, scared and wanting someone to protect her; and in between the two someone...someone who knew everything there was to know about life and even more about death, better than anybody else.

She put her little hand on the edge of the front window.

"Okay, come on, get in."

And then I remembered the time I met her. She was running away from something. Someone must have really shaken her up, because I didn't see anybody and she was still trembling. I began to think that maybe the old lady wasn't terminal, as she said, but instead that some person or persons were chasing her in order to terminate her, that was it, and so that's why she had hired me, so it would look like she had a kind of tough guy who was protecting her. *I have the feeling that someone is always waiting for me, to rape me.* I repeated it to myself twenty times. I was trapped, I really felt that right then, and the worst thing of all was that I hadn't managed to get anything out of the old lady except a few crummy meals. Oh, yes...and a watch. But all of that I wasn't about to trade for my life.

"What are you muttering, Juan?"

"Nothing... 'You have to see where the Devil is leading you to know whether to follow or not.'"

"What does that mean?"

I couldn't think of anything so I just said something or other. She didn't understand that either, but so that she wouldn't look like an idiot, she nodded. She didn't know what the hell was going on. Well, actually, I suspected she did, but I acted dumb and changed the subject.

She wasn't getting in. Holding onto the door right there in the middle of the street, she looked at the prostitutes, then at the sky, then at the buildings, while we went on talking—like she was a street walker from those romantic movies of the forties and I was a good man who was trying to save her from the abyss, or some corny old plot like that.

"Look, the Museum of the City! Have you ever been there, señorita?

"No."

"Well, there should be some queens of the street in glass cases in there, don't you think?"

"That would be the height of immorality!"

No, there was no way she would tolerate such an outrage. Suddenly I saw one of the hookers coming up to the car from my side, that is, from the sidewalk. I was caught by surprise.

"Do you want to come with me? I'll treat you good, like a king. Whatever positions you want are included in the price."

Then the hooker noticed Barbara hidden in the shadow of the Ford's hump.

"Ugh, someone beat me to it!"

"You stupid woman!"

The whore crossed the street toward the old lady.

"Listen, you old bitch! What's your problem?"

"You imbecile! I'm not one of your kind. You harlot!"

I was beginning to enjoy myself. I had never seen her argue so passionately. She actually got the best of the street walker.

"Whore, okay, but harlot…you're not going to get away with that, hija de la chingada."

The queen grabbed poor Barbara with her big white arms, long and covered with blue veins, and gave her what she had coming to her. I wanted to just act like I didn't have a stake in the game, but I felt sorry for the old lady. *If she's going to die now, it shouldn't be painful.* Like a flash I got out of the Ford and managed to separate them, and just then, I saw two pimps getting out of a car; I threw the old lady in the car and away we went.

We left 5 de Mayo Avenue and 20 de Noviembre and we went towards Polanco. The whole way she was blasting away at prostitutes and prostitution until she had reduced them to little grains of shit.

Once, when I had just met her, she told me that some day she would tell me her story, when her memory betrayed her. She said she was from an aristocratic family, from a noble line, a family of the world, with tradition. She didn't have anything much left from all that, except more than enough pride. But that bad woman, what more could she expect from life but death?

And now on a roll with no holds barred, she began to order me around, telling me to turn on streets that no one even knew the names of. "Here. Now this way. Come back up on this one. To the left. Stop. Let's go…"

She got bored and me even more so; both of us were tired. She wound up totally wasted, stretched out in the back seat with her tongue hanging out. I remembered again that business of *There's someone waiting for me, to rape me.* I adjusted the mirror so I could see her. Who'd want to get it on with that crazy old biddy? As for her, the only harm she was doing, she was doing to me and I wasn't complaining. I remembered my mom. They weren't anything alike, except that both were about to die; well, actually, mine was already below ground. Ah…and they both were frightened of everything, and my mom was always, and this one was sometimes, perfectly silent. And that was what I liked best about both of them.

I think that even in her dreams Barbara went on living out the past. One day she told me that someone had said that she wasn't holding onto her memories, she was expiating them. Now I know what that means, because I learned to remember from her, by remembering her.

15

Agustín

WE GOT TO POLANCO at around eight o'clock, and Agustín was already waiting for us, which caused a short circuit in Barbara that totally woke her up. Once again she was like the statue of salt in the Bible.

Agustín stood there motionless. It was waiting for us, or rather waiting for her; what did I matter? We approached along Homero Street and we could see part of its dome and then the curve of it like the back of a dead animal, like the humped back of the Ford and of my VW before that.

It was horrible. She went mad, and without a straitjacket. Barbara twisted around or else the mirror moved in some strange way, but suddenly she was on top of me, her screams pounding my ears. What was this?... What the fuck? She grabbed the steering wheel with her hands and I couldn't see a thing. Everything was whirling around and the car screeched like a wounded elephant. She kept screaming and looking at the temple of San Agustín.

I searched out the brake pedal as best I could with both shoes and the old woman ended up on top of the seat back with one leg on each side. At that hour of the night there was no one around, just me flying out of the car like a shot.

"Crazy old woman! Damn you! We just about crashed. What the hell's wrong with you, anyway?"

I walked away, not caring where, lost among the trees of the park.

"It's my own fault," I kept shouting at myself, "for being such a stupid shit. Do I have to keep putting up with her bullshit? Frustrated, murderous, menopausal old bitch!"

All the while she was throwing screams at me like fast balls: "Juan! Juan! Come back! Please come back!"

I walked on down one of the streets, not wanting to go back. The crazy old woman touched the steering wheel and the gear shift like they were on fire. She managed to start the car and came lurching along and nearly ran me over.

"Shit! She doesn't even know how to drive. Her own car that she makes a living from and she can't drive it. ¡Carajo!

She stopped, or rather the Ford stopped her because it refused to go any farther. The open door looked like a whip snapping from one side to the other. She sat watching me. San Agustín was peeping above the roofs of the wealthy houses, but she didn't see it any more. I kept on walking. Like she thought it was all hopeless, Barbara leaned her head against the steering wheel, and I don't think she knew that that's where the horn button was. The poor thing bounced back and almost broke her neck. I laughed; why not? She got out of the car and closed the door. I saw that she was trembling as she leaned against the hood. At first I thought she was challenging me. But no, she was moving like she was a leaf and the wind was about to blow her away.

I took her by the arm, put her in the car, and then tried to figure out what I could do to make the poor car run.

THE NEXT AFTERNOON, on a lonely street, more or less in the same area, but without Agustín being there, the Ford came jerking along again close to the curb. I wasn't driving. The bitch made me teach her how to drive. She never learned, and she never sat in that place again, not even on the day she died. Her voice, also jerking out of her insides, told me something I couldn't hear because I was busy watching to see when we were going to hit something and smash our faces in.

I wonder what need there was for her to learn. The car was for my wedding, not for her to end up knocking the shit out of.

"The clutch! The clutch! You're going to strip the gears! Put in the clutch!"

"It's all right for you to teach me, but don't talk to me like that. We are not equals, do you hear? What clutch are you talking about?"

I didn't know if she was going to die or if I was going to kill her with all the death wishes I was saving up.

16

A Cup of Tea
with Past, Please

ON ONE OF THOSE AFTERNOONS, Barbara went into the Sanborn's on Lafragua to buy some things at the drug store. I was waiting close to the Madero Street door. Two women even older than her stopped by her side. One took her arm and I heard, "Barbara?"

She didn't recognize them at first.

"Barbara!"—and the first woman turned to the other one—"It's Barbara! Remember?"

The friend didn't say anything and just looked at Barbara, probably because Barbara was younger than her or at least looked like she was.

"Don't you remember me? I'm Leonor and this is Guadalupe."

"Yes. Of course. Leonor and Guadalupe."

"Always together, right?" said the one who talked more.

The other still hadn't said a word. Now she was looking at herself like she was comparing herself in years to Barbara, but then she surprised her friend by interrupting her to say something like, "My goodness! You're looking so well, Barbara! How do you do it?"

"It's been so long since we've seen each other," said Leonor.

"Wait," the one friend cut off the other friend. "Let her tell us what she does to keep herself looking so good."

Barbara kept her secret and Leonor answered the first one, "Yes, we haven't seen her in such a long time."

Then Guadalupe came out with something that sounded like a dig. "Since we two got married."

"Longer," said the one who wasn't Guadalupe, "since before we both got married, because you didn't come to our weddings."

Barbara caught the implication and went on looking for her things. The friends followed her and I moved toward them so I could be closer to all three.

"But tell us," said Leonor, "what have you been doing all these years? Why did you disappear? We all still see each other. Well, not everyone, you know how hard it is in this city, but most of us do, right, Lupa? Where do you live, Barbara?"

"I travel a lot."

"Really?"

"And where do you go?" The other one went on being an asshole, more jealous than ever.

"All over," Barbara answered, like it wasn't very important, but then I saw she wanted to stick it to them. "I swear I didn't recognize you, it's been so long and everything changes so much…"

Guadalupe took this personally and responded with a friendly smile, "True, you're right, but I don't forget a dress even if it's been ages, you know."

Barbara drew in a long, deep breath. For sure she was going to blast them with a swear word, you know, like her usual "Stupid!" but the other one, probably sensing this, changed the subject before the blood began to flow.

"And what do you do, beautiful?"

"Nothing…just live, like everyone else."

"Well, you've still got so much energy, dear!" Guadalupe said.

It wasn't necessary to read Barbara's mind. I think even the other old ladies were aware of how she felt.

"I'm sorry," she said, almost growling, "but I'm in a hurry."

"Of course," was the only thing Leonor could say, "but how about getting together again some time, okay? We all meet here on Fridays. If you want…"

"Don't you see that she's a very busy woman?" said Guadalupe.

"It doesn't matter, one of these days I might be able to get away for a while. Well, hasta luego."

She could have left, I know, or even taken a few steps, whatever; she didn't have to call me. But she did it just so her little friends would realize that she had a chauffeur.

"Juan, take charge of all these packages and wait for the change from my medicine. I won't be long, I'm going to the rest room."

Then she said to the others, "I'll be seeing you…girls."

The way she said it made Lupa and Leonor see buzzards circling over Sanborn's.

Barbara went away to who-knows-where while I waited for the change in the pharmacy. I didn't hear the girls say goodbye, but I did hear them gossiping, because their eyes were following my patrona as she marched off and they didn't realize that I was standing right by their side. I got ready to read their lips because I knew they were going to say something—that was to be expected—but, you know, it wasn't even necessary.

"Good Lord! Things must be going well for her."

Leonor said that. At almost the same time the other one said, "And she travels all the time."

"I wonder how she managed it: her family went broke. Do you remember?"

She had never told me that. Not then, not afterwards either.

"Yes, I heard something about that."

"They were already in bad shape. The mother's family lost everything in Spain. And then her father wanted to marry her off to a politician. That was when we stopped seeing her. I think it didn't work out and she never got married."

"But she must have, because it looks like she's got money," said the jealous one with the same name as the little Virgin of Tepeyac.

"Well, how strange. She's probably a widow. That's why she's wearing black."

"Her husband must have been rich. She was always very money-hungry."

That's when they saw me.

"Buenas tardes," Leonor said to me. She said, "Let's go," to her friend and "Excuse me," to a man across the aisle from her who didn't know her from Adam's grandmother.

I didn't actually see her, but I know that Barbara, in the bathroom, looked at herself in the mirror with some sadness. The friends had made her remember more than she wanted to, and although she'd acted high and mighty, the painful memory of something still stung her. She came back to reality when the ladies' room attendant asked her for a tip. She was glad to pay.

She went out, and now she wasn't in the Sanborn's on Lafragua but in the House of Tiles Sanborn's again. Before she went down the stone staircase that leads to the main dining room, a woman, who'd come out of her crazy head, took her by the arm. No one else in the world was aware of this but her. Later she told me that it was her mother. That's how I knew without a doubt that she was loony, because only crazy people have tea with the dead.

They went down the stairs together, arm in arm, and the Spanish woman must have forgotten the pain of the war because she didn't stop talking.

"My God, woman, it's taking you forever! But you look so pretty, dear! That's how I like you, all dressed up, especially today since we're having lunch with Jorge. You'll see how much he's going to like you. He's a fine young man, very handsome, and a magnificent match. Young politicians have a very good future. You're pretty and even more important, you come from a good family, and don't you forget it, my treasure. We have a name. You were born to be waited on, remember. I'm so proud of you! But don't disappoint us, all right? Behave yourself like we taught you. Oh, if you could only see how much Jorge reminds me of your father when he was young…"

I can't believe that any mother could talk so much going down the stairs of a Sanborn's. It seems to me that Barbara was stuffing a huge piece of memory into a little hole of time, her most beloved treasure box.

On the ground floor, at the first table opposite the stairway, her father and Jorge, her suitor, were sitting. I still didn't know him, just his voice in Barbara's mouth.

"I am absolutely sure," the father said.

"It's not so easy, sir. But there are men in the movement of weight and influence, if you know what I mean," Jorge answered.

"You know you can count on all my support. Since the beginning of the henriquismo movement, we've really been working hard and you know it better than any one. Here come the ladies."

The two phantoms stood up respectfully. The women sat down.

"Jorge was telling me that he's gone through the formalities to acquire a property in those new apartments that they're building in the Condesa district." The father led the conversation right to the point. Then he turned to his future son-in-law. "Barbara's mother and I would like to have the wedding in the San Agustín church, in Polanco. What do you think, Jorge?"

I already had a pretty good idea that that guy was one of Barbara's traumas, and the church was the other, that is, if there were only two, but I still didn't have the whole picture. She would tell me later, when her memory caught up with the Ford at fifty kilometers an hour.

Barbara was sitting next to Jorge. She took his hand and stroked it. Jorge didn't dare to do anything. But the mother noticed it and the kid's hand began to sweat, which didn't bother Barbara in the least. The father kept selling his daughter without realizing that he didn't have to do it.

"I assure you, Jorge, that all the most important families in Mexico will be there."

He gave his wife an affectionate look and said, "All of Spain came to our wedding. It was magnificent!"

While the father's voice and gaze wandered off to the other side of the ocean, Barbara, the one who was remembering all this, took advantage of the opportunity and lifted her future husband's hand to her face and stroked her cheek with it. The mother disapproved of this little maneuver. She picked up the menu and gave it to her daughter so that she would let go of his hand and order her soup of the day. Barbara took the hint and looked at the menu, while her old man went on talking.

"My noble father wanted me to go to Spain to get away from here, from the Revolution. I'm talking about the year 1915. Well, you see, many of my friends did the same thing. Many went to Cuba, others to the United States, one to Paris. I went to Spain, as I said. I met my wife there...and we got married there."

So then it wasn't all of Mexican society but the society from there, I guess. The señora wasn't remembering anything because she had her eye on the kid's hands the whole time, like they were holding the future of the world. The little brat realized it, and while she was choosing between rice alone or with soup, she slowly took hold of Jorge's hand and hid it under the table. Now the one who was sweating was the Spanish lady. The father went on with his bullshit, and his wife had to interrupt him anxiously.

"I'm taking charge of the preparations for the wedding."

Barbara got tired of this long preamble. She was hungry and wanted some pork, but since they didn't let her have it, she looked at the menu again and began to laugh at the prices: enchiladas, one fifty; sopes, seventy-five centavos; glass of milk, five centavos; rice and eggs, one twenty.

"I don't see what's so funny," the mother said.

"It's not important, Mamá."

"So?" replied the mother with her Spanish accent.

"Oh, it's nothing, go on talking, don't mind me."

The mother moved her eyes in Jorge's direction. She didn't move her neck, or her shoulders, or her hands. Embarrassment made only her eyes move.

"Excuse her, Jorge. The heat doesn't agree with this silly girl."

Barbara laughed again.

"That's enough!" her mother had to tell her in the end. Then, pretending to be calm, she said, "My love, I ask you please to behave yourself like a little lady. Like what you are."

"The prices!" Barbara said.

"The prices?" the waitress responded, with an Indios Verdes accent. "Well, the problem is that they just raised them yesterday. Everything is so expensive. What would you like?"

"Bring me an iced tea."

"Sure. Anything else, señorita?"

"No."

The waitress took the menu and looked at it carefully, and finally said, "Well, you're right, they are a little absurd."

SINCE SHE WAS TAKING SO LONG, I went to look for her with the packages and all and I found her having tea by herself. Happy. Very happy. The light from the yellow windows made her look older, her and everyone else. I didn't sit down, I just stood there looking at her. The music from some Ray Coniff record that the record department was promoting helped to make the moment more seductive.

Some time later I commented to Barbara that in that instant it seemed to me that everything moved more slowly, like it was happening in a lost village. She remembered that afternoon perfectly and answered me, "Yes, like in a lost village, where things move to a slow beat, and without histrionics—everyone accepts the futility of life."

17

Gone With the Wind

I PARKED THE CAR in front of Sanborn's by the door that opens onto 5 de Mayo Street. I got out to open the door for Barbara. She climbed in quickly. I closed the door. The traffic got snarled because of me, but so what? I got in and asked her where she wanted me to take her. She just said to wherever I wanted, just so long as it was one of the usual places. I knew the route well. And I did it.

When we ran out of money after a few months, around September, she thought about her mother again. She asked me if I remembered the day in Sanborn's on Madero Street when she had run into some friends from her youth.

"It was in the one on Lafragua."

She didn't even listen to me. She was anxious to tell me that when we left, that is when I opened the door for her on 5 de Mayo Street, she saw her mother in the car. I let her go on. There was no money left; we no longer had anything to do.

"Listen, Juan, I got into the car and I found my mother, whom I had just seen in the restaurant with my father and my fiancé. She said to me, 'I didn't like one bit the way you acted in front of Jorge.' You asked me where we were going and I said to wherever you wished, do you remember? And as soon as you pulled out she spoke to me again:

'I'm talking to you, daughter!' Then I ordered you to go a little faster.
We got to the Paseo de la Reforma, heading toward Las Lomas. 'What
is this lack of decency you showed with your fiancé, eh? You have
made fools of your father and me. Where did you learn such manners, because it wasn't at home, was it? And then that laugh. My
God! So vulgar, and just when your father was talking about the
wedding. Ay, hija, I'm very displeased with you. I'd like to see you
end up single like your Aunt Matilda. We'll see if you're sorry then.'
My mother kept talking. I told you to go faster and we got to the
Periférico, I think it was in the direction toward Satélite. I didn't care
whether you left my streets or not. At that moment it didn't matter
to me. 'I'm talking to you,' my mother shouted. I was beginning to
get exasperated. 'What is the meaning of those little whisperings you
have with him? Answer me. Let's hear it. Confess. Have you had
something to do with Jorge?' 'What are you talking about, Mamá? I
don't understand.' 'You know perfectly well what I mean, don't try to
act dumb.' Ay, Juan, I wanted to tell her it was true, that I had slept
with Jorge, even if it was a lie. I let her suffer for ten seconds. Then I
told her, 'No, Mamá, I haven't had anything to do with him or with
anyone else.' 'Well, I don't know what to think about you any more.'
Faster, I told you. 'I can imagine what he must have been thinking of
you, what he must have been thinking about your father and me.' I
didn't want to listen to her any longer, I couldn't take it any more. It
all seemed the same to me. I opened the back windows, do you remember, Juan? I wanted air. But now...I need it more and more."

I remember that on the Periférico that day a terrible wind started
blowing in through the window Barbara had opened. She kept telling me that the air had turned into a whirlwind in the back of the
Ford and had knocked her over, lifting her dress and airing out her
white legs. She also said that the wind messed up her mother's hair,
and the mother told Barbara angrily to stop playing around, that she

was speaking very seriously. The crazy woman kept telling me to go faster and faster, and even faster, and I remember that I said to her, "We'll see what happens." I pushed the accelerator like I had never done before. I felt the wind blow someone out the window, and it wasn't Barbara. The wind was penetrating her from every direction. I think that maybe it was at that moment that she lost her virginity, and if not, at least she enjoyed it until she had an orgasm.

18

Moral Violations

IT WAS GETTING LATE and it was time to go to the hotel. It was a different one, also in the downtown area. The earthquake hadn't knocked it down. I remember that one day I left a lit cigarette in a crack in the wall to go do something or other. I forgot to go back for it and the wall smoked it. I'm sure that if I'm ever around that place again, the butt will still be there.

I parked the Ford around ten meters from the door. She ordered me to. I was about to get out when she told me to wait a minute. I turned around to look at her but I could only see her legs lit up by the street light, which was the same yellow color as the Sanborn's window. There was a full moon, but the horrible yellow bulb swallowed up all of its silver light. Before, driving around without direction, the white light lit up the night, but it let the night keep being black, and things looked like they're supposed to look at night. All cats were brown. But now, in this light, cats weren't cats anymore and they changed into strange beings. Anyway, I didn't see her face because it was hidden in the rounded back of the car. Those old humpbacks are like forgotten mountains. The ones on a Volkswagon don't even amount to a hill of beans.

"It's been a while since you gave me lessons."

"It's too late to drive right now."

"I'm not referring to those lessons."

"Ah!"

She was talking about learning to read lips. She got out of the car very slowly and walked kind of strangely to the door of the front seat. She stuck her head through the right hand window. She looked like a prostitute. She didn't say a word, then she opened the door and sat down next to me. She had never done that until then. The yellow street light went out. Later it would turn back on again. I've had a lot of women, including passengers, may Laura forgive me. But this time I was nervous. I wasn't scared. I was just nervous.

"There's not much light."

"That doesn't matter."

Then she talked slowly and sweetly. This made me even stiffer. I thought that she was thinking that she was still able to do it.

"Start doing the routine I showed you."

"Which one?"

"The one I showed you the last time."

"I don't remember. The one with the vowels?"

"Yes, that one."

"Ah! I have to touch my lips, right?"

"That's right. If not, the exercise doesn't work."

"A, E, I, O, U."

"But use the tips of your fingers and then imagine that you're seeing your mouth. See, or I mean, feel the shapes you're making. Let's see, do it."

She started. It seemed to me like she was saying something obscene with her lips, but I thought that was impossible, because she didn't even know anything obscene. I did the exercise too and that's when she touched my lips. She told me she didn't have the imagination to be able to see her own. She turned red, then black. The street light went on again and she turned yellow again. Then red again, then yellow, red, yellow, blue, red, yellow, blue, red, yellow, blue, yellow. When I turned to my left, there was a cop and behind him a patrol car with its colored lights.

"Your papers, young man."

"We're not doing anything," I answered the cop; this time maybe I really was scared.

"No!" he said sarcastically. "Of course not."

"It's the truth, we were just sitting here, right, señorita?"

I turn to look at her and Barbara looks at me for a fraction of a second, long enough for me to realize that she's ready to have some fun. Then she lowered her head very demurely, just so the policeman would think that his suspicions were correct.

"You better pay the fine, my love," she said to me—that goddamn fucking bitch—like it was the most natural thing in the world.

The cop noticed my chauffeur's cap.

"Cut the talk and show me your license or I'll take you both to the station right now…" And now I was definitely pissed off.

"You have no reason to arrest us. I was just teaching her how to read."

The officer's laughter exploded in my head, and Barbara's, smothered by her hand, was like acid on the wound.

"That's a good one!" he said. "You're teaching the lady to read, right now, in this light, is that it?"

And in that instant the fucking street light conspired with those sons of bitches and went out. I turned to look at Barbara.

"Señorita, please tell them the truth."

I only heard her giggle again like some stupid-ass mouse.

I decided to get out of the car to see if I could fix things up. I told Barbara not to move, that I was going to solve the problem, and that I had experience with this sort of thing.

The cop took me by the arm and led me over to the trunk.

"It's true, officer, I'm teaching her to read lips."

"With your tongue."

"No. I think you have the wrong idea. She's my boss."

"Well, do it with her if you can, but don't act like a cabrón with me, buddy."

"Don't insult me, either."

"Your papers."

I went back to the car and took out my chauffeur's permit and my driver's license from the glove compartment. She was still laughing under her breath, that damn…

"Here they are," I said to the cop.

Suddenly a voice from the squad car said, "Come on, take him to the station." Then to me he said, "Aren't you ashamed to do your dirty business in the Historic Zone?"

"Listen, this is an outrage. How can you? In this very street there are two other cars and…"

"But their owners aren't here," said the one on the outside.

"So what? Why don't you take their cars?"

"We're not a towing service. We deal with the vehicle owners who violate a…"

"Okay, okay!" I might just as well shut up; I just moved my head, like I was saying *mother-fucking sons of bitches*.

"In the station you can argue whatever you want," said the partner of the first guy and he ordered the other, "Keep his papers."

"Come on, man. Give me a break," I said.

"Call up 2-4 to send out the tow truck," one cop said to the other.

I took a step forward, ready for anything.

"Okay, fine, no problem. But don't take the car… Hey, what do you want to do that for?

"Pick up your papers at the station," one of the two said—it doesn't matter which, they're all alike.

"Give me a chance, don't be… Besides, the regulations say that if you're in the vehicle, then it's all right."

"But this is the Historic Zone, and that's different. We're going to have to go ahead with this."

"But…we can make a little arrangement, if you'd like."

"If you have any complaints, you can report us at the station."

"But, didn't you hear me, mi general? You're saying…"

"I'm saying that it's the role of the authorities to respect the citizens' right to make a complaint."

"No, we don't have a complaint. On the contrary. I know that you guys are cool… So, what do you say?"

"What do we say about what?"

I made a real strange face; you couldn't tell whether I was trying to offer him a bribe or make a pass at him. Finally one of them said, "Well, to help him out and save him the trouble of going to the station, we could…"

"That's it, we could…handle this some other way." I smiled in the dark.

"You know that it's going to cost you more, I mean, to save you all that trouble…"

"Well, don't get carried away," I said to him.

"What did you say to me?" one of them said.

"What did you say to my partner?" said the other.

"No, I mean…" I stammered.

"If you don't like it, you can go make a complaint. It's part of the reform…"

I'd had about all I could take. "About the bribe? Now you can go and complain that the bribe costs too much?"

He got pissed off. "I didn't say that. Besides, you're the one who attempted to incite us to corruption."

"Come on, don't give me that!"

I think that right about then they were going to jump me, the two of them, when one of car doors opened. We heard her feet touch the ground; the top of her head emerged from the hump of the car and then all of her. She went up to the cop and said, "Really, it's too late to be involved in these absurd discussions, and I'm tired. So tell me: what do you want? What's the problem? Quickly, because I want to go to bed."

I felt every hair on my body stand up in terror.

"Get in the car," I told her. "I'll take care of this."

She didn't pay much attention to me, you might say. She waited there, arrogant and defiant. The first cop stood there like an idiot and the one in the patrol car said nothing.

"Señora, it's just that…you two were…" the one outside finally managed to blubber.

"Yes, you got that right, I am a 'señora.' You don't know me but I can prove to you that I am the widow of General, and Congressman, Arteaga, Octavio Artega de los Monteros, and if you continue to bother us, it's going to go very badly for you."

The other guy got out of the patrol car and walked towards us very meekly.

"Arteaga de los…?" he asked.

"I never heard of him," added his partner, the one who had always been outside.

"That's not my fault," Barbara answered. And then to me, "Juan, get your license and take me home, please."

I was about to do that when the first cop said, "Listen, our duty is to ensure morality in the streets."

Barbara was on her way back to the Ford.

"Keep up the good work, officer. Mexico City has become absolutely revolting."

I took advantage of the cop's confusion to take my license from him.

The other one still kept trying, "But what were you two doing parked here in the dark, eh?"

Barbara turned around then and said firmly, "I don't have to give any explanation at all since we've established that we weren't infringing on the law in any way, but out of respect for you, I'll tell you that I have been deaf since birth and I have hired this young man not only to drive my automobile but also to go on teaching me how to read lips. And furthermore, officers, I want you to know that this young man here is my nephew and therefore he is the grandson of General and Congressman Octavio Arteaga de los Monteros. Now are you satisfied?"

As we went on our way, we kept hearing the apologies of those two poor devils on patrol. I couldn't believe it. In no time at all, she had solved everything, and with nothing but the craziest of crazy absurdities. Unbelievable!

Until we got within two blocks of the hotel we drove in silence, but then I busted out laughing when I thought of that crazy woman's wild claims and those fucking cops' incredible stupidity. And my own too.

"If you're the widow of that guy de los Monteros…," I said between laughs, "and I'm the grandson of the famous general…and congressman…then I can't be your nephew…señorita…"

She was flabbergasted for a second. Then she picked up on my mood and started to laugh.

"Ay, that's the first thing…that popped into my head…"

And hahaha and hahaha, like we were drunk on our own laughter, we threw ourselves from one side of the car to the other.

"And besides…" she said between laughs, "if I have been deaf since birth…hahaha, hahaha…"

"How could you have read…my lips…in the dark?" I finished

her sentence with tears in my eyes and my sides aching from laughing so much.

It took a long time before we could stop laughing; then she had to take a pee and we both felt really sleepy.

We almost didn't even say good night to each other before we went into our rooms. Just before I fell asleep I thought that if I was still alive the next day, I was going to be with her again.

19

The Bail Out

YOU THINK you've got things all figured out and no way. How far we were from imagining that after the little affair with the police, those guys didn't laugh at all, but sitting there in their patrol car they mulled the whole thing over and came to the logical conclusion: that we had made asses of them. Hip to the "deaf" lady's game, they had followed us and waited one street behind when we stopped to shit our pants laughing.

What happened was that the next day I'm there knocking on the door of her room all happy and she doesn't answer. I knew she heard me. She was a light sleeper, because of her age, I suppose. I told her I was going to warm up the car in case she wanted to go get breakfast somewhere else. That I would come back up for her in a little while. That she should hurry up. She still didn't say anything. I don't have a good enough ear to hear through doors. The traffic noise had fucked me over in that area.

So I go on out and—what a surprise: the Ford had vanished. Then I was sorry I had insisted on leaving it parked on the street the night before: I was wanting to go to bed and was too damn lazy to put it in the garage.

So what now?

My good mood evaporated and I started spitting onions and garlic. It wasn't hard to figure out what had happened. The police are always watching. I filled up with anger, even at her. *No matter what happens, she always ends up getting me into a bind, the idiotic bitch.* Then I remembered what I had been planning to do to the crazy woman when I got the chance. This time I could do it. I walked down the street like I was walking on air. I felt free. I talked to Laura on the telephone because now I missed her. I told her we'd see each other that afternoon. "I quit that little job I was doing," I told her. The little humpback was waiting for me, but that gave me more peace of mind than the worn out one.

I saw the hotel from far off and thought that she would die soon. Lonely old people and poor foreigners die in no-star hotels.

I stopped on Balderas Street to drink a juice and saw an old car just like the other one go by. It seemed unfair that the government should get something that didn't belong to it. I should bail the Ford out.

I got to the compound for towed cars and paid the fine and all. There was the Ford, with the doors sealed with little paper stickers that would never come off. There was no way to find the sons of bitches who had locked it up. Some guy who was coming for his own car wanted to buy mine. I told him I'd sell it.

"Come see me at this address. I love old cars in good shape and I've been looking for one like yours for a long time."

"Well, what a coincidence! I'll come see you this afternoon."

I called Laura on the telephone to tell her I couldn't see her, that I had one last little bit of business to take care of. She called me a motherfucker. Oh, well.

Then I thought about how you had to have papers to sell a car to a private party and I wasn't even the owner and didn't have any. I could go back to Barbara and take them from her, but it was already really late and for sure by now she had gone out walking somewhere.

I could also go ahead and keep the appointment with the guy and sound him out by saying it was a stolen car. No, I better not. It would be better to say I would get the papers later and ask him to give me something in good faith now, I don't know, maybe even eighty percent of the car's value, and then afterwards I'd bring him the bill of sale and that would be it. Any way you looked at it, that would be better than selling it for parts to a junk yard or on Buenos Aires Street, I said to myself.

I went to his house later. He checked the car out good, all over. He knew something about cars and he offered me big bucks. I said yes right away, without thinking that people don't do things that way. You have to wait awhile at least, I don't know, maybe just to give the impression that you're thinking it over. But I said yes and he asked for the bill of sale. Then I told him the part of my plan that he needed to know, and he suspected that it was stolen. At least he didn't get mad. He simply told me no. I assured him that wasn't the case, and that I would bring him everything that was necessary, but that he'd have to wait a little while.

"All right. I'll wait for you here. You know where I live."

How he wanted to buy the Ford from me! He told me himself that he'd had one of them all fixed up for his wedding day when he was my age. Well, everyone wants to go get married in a car like this. What if the old guy was the old lady's fiancé? I didn't remember what she said her last name was. But no, how could that be? It sounds like an episode from a prehistoric soap opera. Was it turning out now that I would be the butler for those two old corpses, or what?

"Do you know Barbara?"

"Barbara. Barbara who?"

"She's an old señora, well actually an old señorita, who lived in the Santa María de la Ribera district."

"No."

102 / Luis Eduardo Reyes

"Good."

"Why?"

"Nothing. I was just imagining myself as the chauffeur of an old couple from the days of the Conquest."

"How am I supposed to take that, young man?"

I knew it was all stupid because he didn't know what I was talking about.

"Forget it. Let's drop it. It was a private joke. Listen, I'll bring you the papers for the Ford soon."

"Good. I hope so."

I said goodbye and left. Along the way I was thinking about what the old guy was going to say when he was alone—who knows? Maybe: *I have to act dumb with that idiot so that I can get the car. Fine, if he brings me the papers, then it's all well and good.* In other words, I was the one who was the fool. But as I just said, who knows if he said that or not?

20

Returning from the Bail Out

I DIDN'T KNOW what to do. The best thing was to call Laura. But she wasn't in her cave. What an ass I was! Why did I cancel the date? So then what? Should I go get the papers? Go into Barbara's room (if she was still there), slap her around and threaten her into going to the bank with me to get the bill of sale and while we were at it, get the rest of the dough? Or rape her first and then go to the bank? Or do it after we came back from the bank? Or kill her in the attempt and fuck everything and go to the Buenos Aires district? And what if I go to her room and ask her where she wants me to take her and just become her chauffeur again until she dies? And what if she doesn't die or anything? Fucking car! If things kept going like this, I'd just abandon it somewhere and be through with it! That's what I'd do, you know?

I parked it on a seedy corner in the Buenos Aires neighborhood and leaned against a blue door to have a smoke and wait until the local punks stripped it down. More than ten tough characters came up to me, offering to sell me something or looking for anything to buy. I also smoked more than ten cigarettes and the Ford was still there. I crossed the street and checked it out to be sure. Nothing was missing. It even looked nicer than before. The engine: one, two, and it started right up. It went into first without missing a beat and then into second right on time. Third gear, couldn't be better. The brakes were sure and the radio was playing loud and clear. Farewell, my dear young lads!

When I got to the hotel, it was already about eleven o'clock at night. I went by Barbara's room. There was no sound. And I didn't feel like knocking. But what could she be doing? Almost accidentally my hand bumped against the door knob and I opened it very, very slowly. Barbara was combing her long, blond hair. From behind she could still be young enough to be worth going for, but the reflection in the mirror in front of her destroyed all illusions.

I went in and she didn't say anything. She kept her mouth closed and so I couldn't read it. She was biting on three hair pins which she began to put in her hair one by one. I was amazed to see that time hadn't passed for her since I had left her.

Suddenly the crazy chatterbox spoke up: "I'm glad to see you! I was starting to worry. I thought something had happened to you."

I just shook my head.

"Who took the car ?"

"The police from last night."

"But I thought…"

"They wised up to the joke. How could you say such outrageous things?"

"But they let us go…"

"Just so they could get even."

"Well, did they do a lot of damage to the car?"

"No."

"Did you know that this is the first time it's been taken to one of those places?"

"To a compound?"

"Yes."

"I can't believe it."

"You don't believe anything I tell you. You don't even believe that I'm going to die."

" … "

"Never mind. I'm hungry. You too, I bet. Since you spent the whole day going through red tape and all…"

"As a matter of fact, I haven't had anything to eat."

It was odd: she hadn't gotten mad because of the hour or because I had walked into her room without knocking. I felt like her husband.

We went down to the car and the rest was easy. She hesitated before she got in the back seat, but she did it. We went to the VIPS in Chilpancingo. I felt guilty that the Ford had gone to jail for the first time.

21

From One Table
to Another

I PULLED THE CAR into the parking lot. This time she opened the door for herself, without my help. We were walking toward the restaurant when she stopped, looked me over from head to foot like an elementary school teacher and said, "Go back and take off your cap and jacket."

That meant we were going to eat our dinner together. I went back like a little boy on his first date. But then when I thought about it, why? At first I had felt bad about the business with the car and then I felt happy because I was going to eat dinner with her. But I'm a man! How could it be that an old woman was ordering me around at her whim? No. I shouldn't let anyone do that, not even Laura, much less this decrepit old bitch. I came up with a plan. I left the jacket and the hat in the car and went back to her, walking like a real hard guy. In spite of that I had to open the door to VIPS for her, but that would just look like the gentlemanly thing to do, right? She picked out a table and we sat down together. I didn't even ask her for permission.

"Señorita," I shouted, "bring me the menu."

I didn't say *us,* I said bring *me* the menu. In other words, I'm the one who decides. I brought my vieja to VIPS, that's all there is to it. When the waitress brought the menu I almost tore it away from her.

I opened it for me; Barbara would have to peek around the edge if she wanted to see what was on it. I had just decided to have some enchiladas norteñas when, at another table, over by the window, I saw Laura herself facing me. I shit the enchiladas norteñas before I even ordered them, and when Laura caught sight of me, I farted.

Barbara must not have heard anything because she said, "What's the matter with you?"

"With me? Nothing. Why?"

A little while later I noticed that my girlfriend was with a guy that was about two meters tall and looked like a wrestler. My blood boiled, but I didn't say anything. She was staring at me. I decided to talk to her in the way we knew how, so that she could explain what this was all about.

"Do you know her?" Barbara asked.

"Who?"

"That woman."

"Oh, that one. Yeah, she's a friend of mine from bygone days." I slipped in the fancy word so she could see the kind of person she was with.

I waved to Laura, raising my hand quickly, with a nervous little smile, to let them both know that absolutely nothing was going on. The waitress came back to take our orders.

"What would you like?"

"The lady first," I said, now totally embarrassed.

"Please bring me a caldo tlalpeño and some iced tea."

"And for you?"

"Enchiladas norteñas. No, I better not. Just bring me some manzanillo tea."

"That's all you're going to have?"

"I'm not hungry."

The waitress went away with the order and I started the communication with Laura, moving my lips so that she would understand.

I asked her who that guy was. She asked me who the old woman was. I told her I'd explain everything later. She answered that I'd be better off explaining it to my grandma. Me: Why are you being so nasty? Her: Motherfucker again and was the old wreck (that is, Barbara) the little job I had on my hands. I told her that more or less she was, but that I was going to quit, that a problem had come up. The guy she was with never caught on to our silent conversation. Barbara did. And also, who knows how, she figured out that this was my girlfriend and she started flirting with me, the gold-plated bitch, just for the fun of it, but Laura didn't know it.

"Come on, señorita, what's the hang up?"

I was nervous now and told Laura that I'd talk to her on the phone that night so we could both clear up what needed to be cleared up. But Barbara slid over closer to me in the strangest way.

"Ugh, get away from me."

Again I communicated with my girlfriend to explain that she shouldn't pay any attention. And again Barbara caressed my lips lightly, like she was trying to learn the vowels.

"But what's gotten into you, huh?… Can't you see you're getting me into trouble?"

I was putting up with everything for the papers to the car, but that really was too much. My girlfriend's friend turned around and I'm sure he asked her if I was bothering her. She told him no, I could see that. The guy probably said, *Are you sure?* The thing is he was sitting with his back to me and she was facing me and so I don't know for sure what he said, but I think that was it because she nodded her head like she was saying that yes, she was sure. She also told that orangutan that I didn't matter to her any more, and she said it almost mouthing the words so that I would understand it all, even the periods and the commas. And then she went on to say that she never imagined that I'd throw her over for a rich old lady. *But the fool doesn't realize that he's just being used,* she said it like that, with those words. And that I'd be thrown away when I was no longer of use. *He looks like a clown in that uniform.* Ah, so in spite of everything I still looked like a chauffeur, I guess.

Barbara was acting stranger than ever and I ran out of patience, because I was trying in any way possible to get Laura's attention so I could tell her some things. I was beginning to get dizzy, and at one point I said something to Barbara silently, with my lips. And I said, "fucking old bitch," aloud to my girlfriend. In other words, I really screwed up. I saw the guy that was two meters tall, or more, stand up and walk to my table. His shadow covered everything, like in the cartoons. I raised my eyes to the General Electric light bulb, because I knew the good Lord was behind it, but for sure the two of them were both burned out, because everything went black for me. It think it was an incontestable knockout.

THE ALTERCATION got ugly. The night security guard woke up and was about to light into the big guy with his club. The managers tried to calm everything down. The waitresses holed up in the kitchen. The other people…even they noticed it—and remember that the people in VIPS after two o'clock in the morning aren't too wide awake, that's why I like them. They took it all like another order of molletes, which is what everyone has to eat at two o'clock in the morning. Barbara did get scared, but she didn't do anything either. When I could get up, she paid for what we didn't eat and we took off without further ado. Laura stayed there with her big goon and pulled the splinters of my bones out of his hands.

In the parking lot Barbara acted like she was tending my wounds. The inside light lit us up perfectly. There was no other car but the Ford. The two of us sitting close in the front seat. With the rag from the glove compartment—the one I used to wipe down the car when she ordered me to—she was supposedly cleaning the blood off me. But all she did was smear it all over my face because her hands were trembling so much.

"My God! I didn't think it would end up like this. I swear I didn't. Does it hurt a lot? Forgive me, Juan. Tell me how to get hold of your fiancée and I'll explain everything to her, really, I promise. You don't know how bored I… I'm a fool and I always end up ruining everything…"

"Forget it. It's not worth getting all upset about."

"No, because I have to explain something to you. You'll see… I was so bored today in the room waiting for you… No, that's not true, it wasn't boredom, it was…how can I tell you? It was as if I were caught in a roll of film that was being played over and over again, do you see? Horrible! Frightening! Do you understand? No, I don't think you understand me. The truth is that I don't know what happened to me ever since you went to get the car. But in spite of all the anxiety, I knew that you would come back, Juan. No matter how much you wanted to leave me, I knew that you had to return, and when you came into my room without asking permission, you saw how I didn't reprimand you. It was because of that, because I was so happy, very happy that you had come back, do you understand?"

I couldn't believe it.

Then she stopped talking and she remembered something, as usual. She got the same look on her face as she had when she opened the windows of the car so that wind would rape her on the Periférico. So she was seeing something, I'm sure. But at the same time an explosion inside her made a short circuit in her memory. At that moment I remembered San Agustín and the fuss she kicked up when we passed by there.

"Juan." There was no need for her to say another word.

Because I got turned on in a flash too.

22

Where Are You Taking Me, Juan?

"WHERE ARE YOU TAKING ME, Juan? Where do you mean to take me, Juan? Answer me, I'm talking to you!"

To hell with her; I didn't have to answer her. I was the man, I was driving. She was hot and she'd asked for it, hadn't she? Well, then, let her live with the consequences, right? She would get used to not asking me anything. My blood was getting thicker, boiling and pounding in my head and in my prick. She was mine. Mine, what was left of her. Mine, everything that she couldn't give me any more. Accounts would be settled. Enough of all that fucking torment! It was just a few more blocks before we would finally see how things stood with us.

The hump of San Agustín poked up again over the flat roofs of the houses in Polanco. It was like the Ford's hump, but way bigger, like God's must be. She went crazy all over again. I knew that would happen, that's why I had brought her. When we were driving behind the church, she grabbed me without warning. I could barely control the steering wheel. We turned into a street going the opposite direction and now nothing could stop us; we began to go round and round like lunatics. The inside light was on, and we must have looked like demons flying around the church. She was hitting me and shouting

like she was being exorcised. She punched me in the face and I grabbed
hold of clumps of her blond hair while I ground her face against her
window. She looked red to me, maybe because of the color of her
lips. As much as I tried, I couldn't laugh at that flattened face…

We went round and round, circling that thing, until the car started
lurching, making us move like I moved in bed with Laura. Smoke
was coming from somewhere, but I didn't let go of Barbara's hair. Then
steam started escaping from the car and I couldn't see anything else.

When the Ford died (because I hadn't spent the money for its
upkeep), it was in front of the church. That was the perfect place,
because right there was the center of her pain, that was where the
mystery was hidden. *Let's see if your bite is as good as your bark,*
I thought. As for me, I had nothing to lose, because if I lost with her,
I'd have a chance to get myself back. And if on the other hand, I won
out over the old lady and her ghosts, even if I was condemned to her
hell, even if I lost everything, at least I would have rid myself of
loneliness forever. So, why not? I had to, right? It was one more
tradeoff, like everything in life.

She tried furiously to shake off my hands. I let her go. She gave me
one last blow to the chest, awkward and almost absent-minded. She
stumbled out of the car, and almost fell, but she got her balance back
in a flash. And suddenly…suddenly, she was transformed! Dignified,
calm, and haughty, she walked up to the door of the church. The
poor thing was smiling. That bitch was happy! She had gotten her
way. She'd won the battle; she'd stuck it to the dead folks!

I got out so I could see better through the smoke that was making
everything gray. She got to the closed door and knocked on it with
her little hands, and a wooden echo resounded in the souls of the
saints. Then she talked to someone, herself, because no one was there.

She came back to the car, almost running, leaving whoever it was
just standing there.

She took my hand. She got into the back seat first, then I did. Through the windows I saw tattered images of human beings…

AND THE LOVE MAKING was different. Different, only because we could never possibly have imagined it that way. Splashing in our own blood, we plunged to the very bottom, until we died; although Death was still sitting in her place in the Ford—like a grandmother resigned to waiting—dozing off, nodding in the lull of someone else's dream.

I heard a drop of rusty red oil drip stubbornly from the chassis, like to prove without a doubt that this was the first time.

PART TWO

Resurrection Sunday

23

The New Life

EVERYTHING WAS CLEAN, shining, smelling like a morning in a technicolor movie. I expected to hear music coming from somewhere or other. I was fixing the Ford's engine. Barbara wasn't there. She had gotten up early and gone to buy some things.

A crazy old woman—who wasn't Barbara—was standing beside the church door. She poked her head inside, and then she looked at me, and then prayed, "Let them come out. Aren't they ever going to come out? They'll stay there forever: the Lord has taken them away." And she peered into San Agustín. "Let them come out, sweet Christ. Hurry up, I'm so hungry."

Just then a woman and her two very virginal daughters came out, like they were appearing on a color screen. The old woman reaches out her hand asking for charity, but the women don't even see her.

"God didn't forgive that woman," she said to me. "I know, that's why they didn't pay. I come here after Mass, which is when the sinners pay for their sins by giving me money. Yes. At first I used to be in the Plaza, in front of the City Hall. There you have to get the poor souls before they enter, because that's when they have money. They come out a little later the same as me, without a centavo to their names. I don't even bother to go to the police station."

I had blown a hose. I was fixing it when Barbara showed up with her packages. She left them in the car and said, "Hurry up. We have to go to Mass."

"What?"

"To Mass. Hurry up. You can finish later, let's not be late."

"Listen, I'm not going."

"You're not going? But, why? You don't believe in God anymore?"

"He's the one who doesn't believe in me. And that's even though I'm a Catholic."

"I know that. Come on, we're going anyway."

"But what for, man!"

"We have to give thanks."

"For what?"

"For...for being alive."

"But He's just about to kill you..."

I knew I'd better just shut up, and we went on into San Agustín.

24

It Wasn't the Right Moment, and What's That?

NOW, INSTEAD OF LOOKING at her mouth, I looked at her eyes and then at them, the figures of the saints. They accused and she challenged. What had happened last night in the night didn't matter to her. She was there to pray, like every other Sunday. Before, I would wait for her at the entrance, but now she made me go in; I wondered why. Of course! It was because I wasn't her chauffeur any more. Now I was a person.

I was in a church. But anyway, if that damn old lady thought that because I had screwed her... I was in a church...last night... Does this mean that because of that she's not going to pay me any more? What a crock of shit!

I interrupted her in the middle of a prayer to ask her when she was going to pay me my wages for the week. At first she didn't pay any attention. I asked her again. She acted like she was in a trance. I asked her a third time. She pointed to the front, as if God were up there saying Mass. After the fourth time she answered that this wasn't the right moment. At this point in our relationship I was calling her "tú" and we could say anything to each other. I asked her again.

"We'll see about that later. Now you should be repentant."

That was all she said and I was repentant, but because I regretted what had happened between her and me. From now on I wouldn't know how she was going to react.

I waited until Mass was over and then we left. I didn't say anything. Out of respect, maybe. We went straight to the Ford. I didn't open the door for her anymore but I kept looking at her to find out what she wanted. Well, actually, I did still open the door for her, but it was the front door, just like any other son would open the door for his mother after Mass. By the time I went around to my side and got in, my mother wasn't there any more. Suddenly she appeared in one of the windows, wiping the car with the cloth. Good, at least I'd gotten something out of all of this. I told her to get in. For the first time in all the time that I had known her, it seemed to me that the Ford wasn't the Ford but something else, and later I would find out what.

After a while she had to get out because she was dizzy. I was even more worried about the money. I got out and got her back in again. I had to ask her for the money before she croaked on me.

"I just got dizzy, I'm okay now."

"It's not good for you to run around so much," I said to her like we had been living together for a long time.

"Don't worry, it's okay."

I let four or five cars go by without saying anything and then said, "Barbara, it's the end of the week, and so…"

"It's the end of the week, and so what?"

"So…"

"I know. I have to manage the money better now, so we've got enough to make ends meet. Everything is so expensive these days."

"Don't tell me that you're not going to pay me any more!"

"Don't say 'pay,' honey."

"And don't you call me 'honey.'"

"Here."

Barbara took the money from her purse. She had some left over; I liked that.

"This is for whatever you need. I think I can manage to cover the week's expenses, my love."

I was hoping, and I told her so, that she wouldn't treat me like that, and I also said that I didn't give a damn about the cost of living as long as she kept paying me what we had agreed on.

She kept feeling dizzy and I kept insisting that she pay me, so she would see that she couldn't get out of it by making me feel guilty because she was acting sick again. I asked her coldly if she was about to turn up her toes. She answered that I shouldn't be so mean to her, that I should have a little consideration for her. I really suspected that she was screwing me over, the crazy bitch.

"I think you're trying to manipulate me."

She told me she wasn't, that I should at least consider the possibility that she might be pregnant. That really made me laugh. She was out of her head. She came back at me with, "Why else would a woman get married or have a husband?" What she wanted was to get me in her clutches but she wasn't going to succeed. I was getting tired of this because she kept harping on it and I kept wanting to drop the subject.

"I can't take it any more!" I said. "Let's give it a rest."

"Sure. That's the way you all are. As soon as you get what you want, you leave."

Where had I heard that before? Well, in all the Mexican movies made the same year as the car. Then from all the abandoned mothers in the city. There was even a verse about them: "Poor abandoned women, who go through the world remembering a child and dragging a man around," or something like that. And now Barbara was saying it. It seemed to me that things were going in a direction I didn't like at all. How far I was from realizing that she was just playing the part of an actress; she was being Marga López or Libertad Lamarque or Lilia Prado or Charito Grandos, or someone like that. After all we'd been through together, I still didn't really know my old lady.

"Poor woman who believes everything a man tells her."

"You know you wanted it too yesterday, you can't deny it."

"Because I thought there was something more."

"Like what?"

"How have I failed you, Juan?"

"Ay, don't talk to me like that, we're not married."

"How things have changed…!"

"Barbara! Come on! Stop it! If you're going to go on like this, I'll see you around. You can keep everything. I don't give a damn. I'd prefer it. Adiós."

I put my left foot on the ground and she put her right hand in the glove compartment. Time stood still as we stared in each other's eyes, each waiting for the other to blink. I blinked and she took out the bill of sale for the car. My foot was still outside. When she began to endorse the bill over to me I acted offended but I didn't say anything. She looked at me and didn't say anything either. I brought in my left foot trying to make her think that I had changed my mind on my own and not because of what she had just done. I let three cars pass us before I spoke again, but then I saw an old hard bound notebook in the glove compartment. And just like that I changed the subject.

"What's that?"

Barbara put away the bill of sale and took out the notebook.

"A diary."

"A what?"

"A diary…don't you know what a diary is?"

"But no one has one of those any more."

"That's what you think. Things have a way of coming back."

"All that corny shit that…" She shut me up with a look. *Oh well.*

"In my day it was very common for all the girls to keep a diary."

"You said it: 'in your days.'"

"I don't see anything wrong with it. And besides, the boys also kept diaries."

I was still thinking about the papers for the car, but I had made her talk and change the subject and that was good. I didn't care about her memories or her present thoughts or whatever: the car was now legally mine, although that same afternoon she told me again silently with her lips that she wanted to go to the bank. Legally it was mine, but now the papers were in the bank. In other words, I was bound to her out of pure illegality!

Dear Diary: Today, after many years and much remorse, confusion and fear… I find you again at the very moment that I find life again! I am incredibly fortunate. I'm going to tell you a secret: I'M IN LOVE!

In order to write again in that diary which had been closed for more than forty years, I imagine that that night, in the hotel, Barbara had to become 18 years old again.

Later I realized that that wasn't true. That she always wrote in a different way, as if on each page she became a different person. I think that from this mix of personalities came the glue which kept me together with her.

I licked my finger and leafed through about twenty pages, stopping at one which had the same date as the one I had read before. This one was some bullshit which I didn't understand but which got confused with one of my dreams, one that keeps coming back all the time—that one, the one I can't remember ever.

I hardly ever dream when I sleep. Last night I had a dream which I forgot when I woke up. But the feeling it provoked has stayed with me.

Or I should say, the NON-feeling. It was as though I were without life, suspended in the void, waiting for something definitive. No, it wasn't for death, dear Diary; rather, I was waiting for what might have been the fulfillment of a promise made long ago and forgotten. I wasn't thinking of who had made me the promise; that was not at all important. The importance lay in that enigmatic possibility which I was waiting for. What I do remember perfectly is the moment before I fell asleep, when I turned off the light and thought about what I had done with my life. But my empty eyes saw only darkness...

I read it twice and couldn't believe it: for the woman who wrote this, I was a stranger. She didn't even mention me! I didn't exist. How many old ladies and young ones, women and little girls were there in Barbara? How many were going to die? Which ones loved me?... In other words, who were we, she and I?

I wonder.

25

Menopause of Nostalgia

AFTER WE GOT GAS, Barbara felt better, and I did too, somewhat. These days the only part of the chauffeur's uniform I had to wear was the pants, and since they were gray I could pass for a government worker. She sat in the front seat and that lifted the burden of being a chauffeur, but it added another: her full seventy-two years.

I asked her why I shouldn't just drop her off at her house. She reminded me that she no longer had one. Nothing was left but the car and hotels.

"Okay, but why don't you go and live with a relative? Don't you have a brother or sister, a cousin, or anyone at all?"

She had no one left. I should have asked her about that before; it was a little late now for me to come up with a different plan. The truth is I didn't know what to do, although she did, very well.

I think she took me for her husband. We were newlyweds and she wanted to flatter me in her way, and her way was nostalgia. The first thing she did was to take me to the Alameda Park, and to get there we had to take a detour, because there was a demonstration. When we got there we looked like outdated demonstrators with useless

truths. We sat on one of the benches and she told me that when she
was young she would come to the Cine Alameda with her mother to
see matinees and live performances. Everyone went to see them, she
said. "There were so few of us…"

"If we didn't come here," she went on, still stuck in that era, "we
went to the Cine Cosmos to cry our way through Doris Day films.
I know what we'll do! You'll see, we're going to have a great time."

"What?"

"Just wait. You'll see."

Before we left the Alameda to—as she said—"have a great time,"
we left behind a hustler who was conning the people with a line
about the menopause of manliness: "I'm not here to take your money
or to sell you anything. I'm here thanks to this manual that changed
my life. I used to be a coward, a frightened man, or should I say, a
common bum. But now I ask you, I beseech you, would a coward do
this?" And he stabs an ice pick up his nose.

Barbara took me to a place near by, in the Plaza Colón, to a spot
she said used to be called Randesvú, where young people would meet.
But all we found was a travel agency. She told me not to give up, that
the Hotel Reforma was right across the street and surely there was
still a Kikos there.

"A what?"

"A café where people go to listen to music."

When we went into the hotel an employee said the same thing I
had: "What?" And then: "If you're looking for the restaurant, it's on
the ground floor to the left."

Barbara began to lose heart. Maybe she didn't tell me so, but I read
it, not on her lips but later in her diary, one night when I couldn't sleep.

And then she invited me to go to a jai alai game at the Frontón
México, and as we passed by the Alameda the hustler was still
going on:

"This will show you the prodigious miracle this manual has worked in me. I'm not here to sell you anything, don't worry about that; I only want to bear witness..."

When we got to the Frontón it was closed due to a strike that had begun many years ago.

One other afternoon she invited me to go to the Cine Cosmos, because she said she used to go there with her friends to cry their way through the Doris Day films. When we passed by the Alameda the hustler still hadn't given up:

"Look at me, señores, I'm not handsome, I'm not attractive, I'm far from being a pretty boy. The ladies never even turned to look at me out of pity. But now I pluck any rose in this garden, thanks to Dr. J.P. Mayer's manual and thanks to its secret weapon: the 'Pppsiqui secs master.'"

When we got to the movie theater, Doris Day wasn't there, but the Ninja Americano was. That afternoon was totally cool for me, you can bet.

One morning she made me leave the hotel early to go to the Bahía Bath House in the Zaragoza district, because it would be too crowded later. We drove past the Alameda and that guy was still going on:

"Thanks to this manual I found confidence. You, or you, come on, confess to yourself, in secret, your failures. Dare to be different, señores, not like every Tom, Dick and Harry you see on the street. After all, think how you have everything Jorge Rivero has..."

When we got there we didn't find the Bahía either. It had been closed. No one ever went there. Then she really did feel bad and just wanted to go back to the hotel and sleep.

On the return trip past the Alameda I could just manage to hear:

"In just seven days, señores, with this manual, you could even get a queen. Don't waste time and useless effort. This is a great opportunity for you to seduce the opposite sex in an instant."

But that night she felt the nostalgic pull again and we went to dance at a dance hall called the Waikikí, near to where the Caballito used to be.

"Here you can learn the scientific secrets of sexual magnetism: One, you will gain control of your psychic abilities and attract women. Two, you will control from a distance the will of the women you desire."

When we got to the place, it was a diner. That was it; she couldn't take it anymore. She didn't say a single word. Neither did I. I started up the car and we went back to the hotel. I don't know why but I felt like making love to her. It was one of those times when you want to do it more for the other person than for yourself. But she didn't want to. I never thought nostalgia could be stronger than passion.

The next day she woke up in a good mood because she still had a little nostalgia left over. She wanted to go to the bull fights. She told me to go to the Condesa district. There aren't any there, I told her, but she didn't pay any attention.

"Come on, let's go, so I can relive the times when I used to go there with my papá."

Instead of a bullring we found El Palacio de Hierro department store. We didn't even buy anything because everything was so expensive and life no longer permitted us such luxuries. I laughed, not at what had happened to us but at the hustler's last words:

"For the same price, señores, and just in case the manual doesn't work, included with it comes the pyramid of the Egyptian gods, which always brings good luck. And if you don't believe that, why do you think the dollar is always going up while the peso goes down? It's because on the back of the dollar is the pyramid of good luck, while on the other hand our peso just has pictures of heroes."

We ended up drinking coffee in the Sanborn's in El Palacio.

26

Laura, Laura, Laura

I WAS WRONG; we didn't end the day at Sanborn's. We had coffee there, that's true, but then we went to the scenic overlook above the city. The same one she had taken me to before. The lights from passing cars lit us up. We stayed there a long time without moving. It was impossible to go back. I felt sad; well, no matter. It was no longer the same city it had been the other night. Now the old lady was nostalgic about her earlier nostalgia.

I was tired. I demanded that we go back to the hotel. The only things that mattered to me were sleep and Laura. I don't know why I was thinking about her so much then.

Without a word she got in the car and waited. I shouted, "To the city!" and an echo sounded somewhere. (For anyone who may have heard it.)

We came back via Tlalpan or one of those avenues in the south that look like landing strips. We got back quickly to the center of town.

A block away from the hotel, Barbara asked me to wait for her, because she wanted to buy some medicine at the druggist's. "Druggist" —I hadn't heard that word in a long time.

While she was buying the medicine, I took advantage of the moment to talk to Laura on the phone.

"Listen, what's with all this hostility? Tell me why."

"Don't act dumb. You know perfectly well why I call you that. And anyway, it's over."

"Don't be like that. What do you mean, 'It's over'?"

"Just what I said: it's over."

"I'm making money, Laura. Whatever it is, for her or for me, the old lady pays. Besides, she just signed over the car to me, I mean, it's already mine, legally, but I still don't have it yet because it's something that I'll explain to you later. I'm telling you the truth."

"Look, I don't care."

"Okay, what do you want me to do? Just tell me."

"Do whatever the hell you want to. Why don't you marry her?"

"You see? You're jealous. Before you didn't want any of that with me, but if now you want me to do it with somebody else, then you do care. You see?"

"Don't give me that shit! Just wait a while and you'll see that you will wind up marrying that old mummy."

"Now you don't give me that shit. You're as crazy as she is."

"Yeah, right. Okay, then, why don't you leave her? Just because she pays you a lot? Yeah, sure. Come on, ask yourself. Come on!"

"Come to think of it, you owe me one too. Who's that little gorilla, huh? Don't tell me you think that just because he caught me off guard, he can survive the ass-kicking I'm going to give him, huh? Come on, answer me that, why don't you?"

The phone was silent for a while. Then Laura hung up.

"Listen to me…!"

I heard the horn of the Ford.

"Laura, Laura, Laura!"

It was Barbara who was calling me. Let her wait. I dialed again, but no one answered this time. I slammed the phone down. Something was moving near the metal curtain. I couldn't make out what it was. It was moving and making choking sounds. It dragged itself toward me. I saw an eye and spit at it. There are things in the Centro that no one knows what they are. And then I went to the Ford; what else was there for me to do?

DEAR DIARY: Self-sacrifice is a quality that ennobles women, my mamá used to say. But I'm not self-sacrificing: maybe I'm not even one of those women who can hold on to a man… The other night he talked to someone on the phone. I was dying of jealousy. Then of shame. I don't know why I love him, but all the energy I have left I'm spending on loving him. I confess, dear Diary, that I still believe in the miracle that he will fall in love with me. This will be my last fantasy in my life… How awful is the fate of people who long so for what can't be, for what we are not, for what we can never have! As long as hope lasts, our existence is painful, but without hope, why would we want to exist?… I have to learn to be self-sacrificing and to suffer in silence because if I don't, the reality will be unbearably grotesque: I'm about forty years older than he is…! I'm like a thirsty animal that has gotten used to drinking from dry water troughs…

"WHAT'S GOING ON? Who were you talking to?"
   "No one."
   "I'm not a fool and I won't allow you to lie to me."
   "All right, that's enough, okay?"
   "Weren't you in a hurry to get to the hotel?"
   "Whose idea was it to stop at the 'druggist's'?"
   "Because I'm sick. Because I'm dying! But that doesn't matter to you one iota…! How would you know what it's like to die day by day if you never even grew up, if you only managed to become a pathetic little neighborhood punk?"

I got pissed off.

"I may be a little neighborhood punk, but that's who you got involved with! And listen, I do know what it's like to die day by day, stupid!"

I paraded all my sufferings before her eyes. I showed her everything from the scars on my ankles to the wounds on my head, pointing out along the way the broken bones you couldn't see. That was my pay for having made it to the age of twenty-some years, without counting the hunger and the desperation. And she still had the nerve to tell me that I didn't know anything about death. If death was talking in her ear, it was pounding me into the ground.

I grabbed her by the hair at the back of her neck.

"Barbara, aren't you afraid that I might drag you out of the car? That I'll take everything you own? That I'll say to hell with you and leave you all alone to wander crying up and down the streets? Look...it's nighttime...no one is here, just some thing that's crawling along under the chassis. I could even kill you! Barbara, hasn't that ever occurred to you?"

She was quiet. Then she said, "I don't think you could do that."

"Why not?"

"I can see it in your eyes."

"Spit in them!"

"What?"

"Ay, stop acting like an idiot! You're like out of a soap opera."

"Don't put romantic movies in the same category as those junky soap operas."

"Look, Barbara, I'm a son of a bitch. And you are...I don't know... Jesus! Sometimes I even feel sorry for you!"

I let her go. I don't know why, but I really felt like crying. What the fuck!

My legs were hurting like I had just run all the way to Cuernavaca on one foot. It was some kind of godawful tiredness—deep inside me.

"Hey, man, what's happenin'?"

I turned to the window and saw a guy who was younger than me, and darker.

"What's up, man?" said another guy, who was definitely even blacker, from the window on Barbara's side. And the blackest of all of them was waiting behind the 614 AFJ. I moved my eyes and the lightest one said, "Stay cool, sonny boy. Get out of the car. Come on, Blackie," he said to the one who was on Barbara's side, "You take charge of the lady."

The guy who was really black stayed by the trunk. The first one spoke again, "Behave yourself if you want to get out of this with your ass in one piece."

"The old lady's not too bad-looking," said Blackie.

"Come on, take whatever the old bitch has," said the one from behind, from the trunk. "And you too. Get moving!"

Turned toward the window, I stretched my arm back to cover Barbara's waist and managed to say, "Listen, no, wait. There's no reason to…"

"Shut up, cabrón!" He pointed something at me that looked like the eye of a gun barrel. "Or I'll blow you apart with one of these little BBs."

"Hurry it up!" said the blackest of those sons of bitches, who was still standing behind the car. I wished that that thing I'd seen under the car would come out and eat them up piece by piece!

"Come on, hand it all over. Starting with that nice little watch…"

2:31 and two seconds was the last I saw of it. Afterwards, there was no more time and I had to give him what I had.

"I like those nice little pants, too…hand 'em over…don't you understand? Come on, let me have 'em."

"Fuck," I muttered.

"Son of a motherfucking bitch! What the fuck are you waiting for?"

"I'm not going to take them off."

"What do you mean?" To Blackie, he said, "Take the old lady, she's yours."

"You leave her alone!"

"Well, just stick around and you'll see what we do to her."

Blackie began to drool on Barbara's neck. She was paralyzed with terror.

"I said, leave her alone or…"

"Or what, asshole?"

"Listen, man, you can do whatever you like to me, but leave her out of it."

"Your pants."

"I just told you that I…"

"Tough little fucker, huh?…well, they're coming right off."

The blackest of all of them came close and told me to knock off the bullshit, and if I didn't, he would take what he had in his hand and stick it in me; and furthermore, he was going to take my pants off. But the first one said no, that I had to do it all by myself. Then he said, "Get on with it."

"I'll get you for this."

I couldn't hear anything from Barbara. I could just see that the one they called Blackie was on top of her. I tried to get over there, but the really black one knocked the wind out of me with a fist in the middle. I fell and slammed my face against one of the tires. I heard the "psss" of a punctured tube and a little puff of air hit my nose and made me sneeze with no air in my gut. The first guy picked me up so I would take my pants off myself. I took them off, totally humiliated. They shit their pants laughing.

"Let's go," said the black guy. "The cops'll be by soon."

It occurred to the guy inside the car that the Ford was worth taking too. All my capital was about to disappear. Even without my pants on, I reacted like a man, but this time a bang on the head with a pipe sent me to the ground again and I felt the little breeze up my nose. I heard something like "the keys," "Get the old bitch out of there," "Turn it on," "I can't," "Pendejo, let's get out of here." The black tennis shoes (I even thought I recognized them because they looked just like those shoes that were chasing Barbara when I let her in my taxi for the first time) bounced away in the night from a Centro so small that anything was possible there.

Underneath the car I got a look at that thing before it pissed in my face.

27

"Dear Diary"

I DIDN'T CARE that the next day I would have to fix the flat tire. Or that after the attack, Barbara would get me another pair of pants in the hotel. And much less that they hadn't stolen the Ford, because Barbara had flipped the security lock just in time.

The only thing that mattered to me was that Barbara would think I was man enough and that I wasn't afraid of anyone. And that if they had taken me on alone everything would have turned out different. The night of the robbery I made love to her like I had never done it before, not even with young chicks. You know, to drive home the point that without any doubt I was all man.

Smoking a cigarette afterward (me, because she didn't smoke), I told her how it was: "I want you to know something."

"What is it, mi amor?"

"I don't like anyone to think I'm a wimp. Because I know that's what you're thinking, don't try to deny it."

"No, I didn't think anything."

"I could have taken care of myself alone if you…if I'd been alone when they jumped me…bam!

"All right, forget it. It's over."

"No, it's not over. The pants. How do you think I felt, huh?"

"But they're just a bunch of punks. They didn't take anything important."

"It seems like I can't think of anything but that."

"What?"

"What do you mean 'what'?"

"And all this you're telling me, when did you think of it?"

"Touch me here, touch me. Two bumps on my head."

"Yes, you already mentioned that."

"Another knife wound on my leg, look…broken ribs, feel them."

"You haven't answered me, Juan. When did you think about all this?"

"Just now."

"When we were making love?" And here she started acting strange. "It's perfectly clear you were only working all this over in your mind instead of feeling anything, of feeling me."

She twisted her lips and lowered her eyes, sulking.

"No. Right now is right now. And right now it weighs like a ton on me that you don't think I'm a real man."

"But, what were you thinking about when we were making love? Tell me that."

"You're so stubborn. That's what I was thinking about, that we were screwing, what else?"

"Don't use that street language with me."

"Or any other language either, because it's impossible to talk to you."

She looked at me with narrowed eyes, like she was sizing me up. I could tell that another blow up was coming, one of the ones that only women understand.

"I give myself fully to you, but all you know how to do is lie and lie and lie…"

"Barbara, okay, stop it!"

She got up furiously and put on nothing but her robe. Then she spoke softly, but with daggers: "The truth is that you're just a poor devil. You're phony to the marrow of your bones."

"What do you mean, phony? And these scars, what are they? They're my tip for ten years of beating the streets. Go on. Tell me again I'm a phony. Go on."

By now she had sat down at the foot of the bed and started to punish me.

"I too was thinking about something else when you were making love to me. And believe me, I don't know where you get these big ideas about yourself."

"Yeah, sure, as if you were young enough to make anyone lose his head over you, right?"

"Think what you like, but I swear to God, even the boys who robbed us would have given me more pleasure."

More than anything else, when she said that about the "boys" it pushed my button. I wouldn't even have taken that from Laura. As far as that goes, not from anyone who wears a skirt. The old woman wanted a war and she was going to get one.

"Besides being old you're stupid, because without even liking me you keep me tied to you. Why don't you let me go? Answer me that."

"Because a woman gets married for the first day, even though the rest are a continuous disappointment. But no matter. That's my cross to bear, not yours."

"Well, now that we're talking about it, let me tell you that I'm so bored in bed with you that every time we do it I have to turn myself on by thinking about doing it to some fine young chick."

"And I with movie stars, not with some poor chauffeur that I'm paying."

She went to the dresser and took out another purse that I hadn't seen her with before and bills appeared.

"There you are. You're paid."

And she threw the money on the bed. I didn't know what to do;

but it was money and whatever else, money is still money. I took it and hid it under the sheet. When I looked up there was Barbara looking thoughtful, with her mouth all twisted to the side, and that always meant something bad.

"How lovely," she said. "I pay you. It's exciting, isn't it, to pay for that? I hadn't thought of that before. It feels strange."

She untwisted her mouth and I noticed that she was breathing more normally.

And then she smiled, turning into a naughty little girl.

"All right, now you. You pay me. Come on, pay me."

"Oh sure. You! What you really want is for me to give you the money back."

"No, no. Then I'll buy you again and that's it."

"I don't believe you."

"So that you know how it feels too. Come on."

I looked at her and she really turned me on. I wanted to treat her like a whore. Then I remembered the time we were driving past a corner and how she looked at the whores. One time a passenger I was taking to the University told me that all women have a whore in them. I don't remember why he told me that then... Now I remember! I slugged him in the middle of Insurgentes Street when he told me that also every man has a faggot inside him; you bet I slugged him, because I knew what the fucker was leading up to. I think Barbara had found her whore. Did this mean the guy was right and so then every man...? No! No fucking way. I took the money out from under the sheets and threw it on the floor.

"Take your pay in advance!"

"No, not like that."

"So, how?"

"Throw it at me."

I liked that idea. I took the money from the floor and I threw it at her body. A twenty peso bill flew free and hit her in the face. I think that's what made her laugh.

"It's your turn again."

She gathered up the bills and threw them in my face. I liked them all. Before I stopped seeing the pictures on the bills, she threw herself too.

"You're mine as long as I pay for you."

"You're demented."

"If you're not mine, you die."

"You're a fool."

"You may keep on eating and sleeping and walking, but I swear to you, Juan, that when I die you're going to die too."

DEAR DIARY: Nothing is more fragile than reality. Think of it, who would have believed that at this age I would be playing erotic games with a boy and that I would be describing them on your pages that for my whole life have remained blank? Isn't it incredible? And the most inexplicable thing is that I'm happy, that guilt has been crushed to death by a brutal and primitive freedom that goes beyond reason. When everything indicated that I would die that way, virgin, dried up, rotten, I have managed to know pleasure. I have learned that sex can become as sublime as spiritual love. Because of that, when both occur and intertwine we achieve the only reality worth living, even though it be only one time, even though it be for just one moment in eternity... Who would dare tell us what we are going to be? Not even our own deepest voices can foretell it. It's because time changes us, time and its circumstances, as they say. What links me now with that Barbara in love with that young politician? How I would love to know! How I would have liked to sleep with Jorge, and with others, to know the size and shape of love. Juan has been and will be the only man of my life. Love before death. Perhaps because of that, true love... Perhaps... As for him, I know now that he finds me desirable and that he'll never admit it to me. This overshadows my

happiness a little. Words have always been important to me. I love them.
I need to hear everything important in words, in precise words that can
project what another feels... Still... Later I have seen him get up. I
pretended to be asleep. He sat near the window and I think it must have
been for at least an hour. Immobile. He seemed to be afraid. Then he
found you, dear Diary.

I WROTE: "Dear Diary..." "Dear Diary..." "Dear Diary, I don't
know how to say things. I think them, but I can't write them." I
scratched it out.

Now I was writing a diary! I couldn't do it, even though I started.
Don't make fun of me, I only did it for her. "Dear Diary, I think..."
No, that's not how you do it.

I gave up. If I couldn't tell her I loved her in bed and that she was
a marvelous woman, I should at least write it in my diary. But there
was no way. I was locked up tight. How could I explain to her that
when she held me I felt her years cover me as if I were covered by all
the lovers on earth? The idea came to me but when I took up the pen
it flew out of my head. At other times I felt very sad. She had said it:
I was nothing but a poor chauffeur. And on the other hand, she was
way over the hill; she could even be my grandmother! It seemed
ridiculous to keep it up. There was no road for us. That's why I
decided I should leave, but right away—without thinking about it,
because if I did the desire would return and maybe even more strongly.
Okay, that's it, let it be. Take it easy. *Let her keep everything, the money*
and the car, what do I care? I said to myself.

I took the page where I had written "Dear Diary." I crushed it into
a ball and threw it out the window. I had hardly thrown it when I see
the black guys with the tennis shoes of the same color walking along
totally unaware. Goddamn! How could I pass up the chance to get
even? When I reached the sidewalk I just had time to look at the

wrinkled paper on the ground. I don't know why I looked at it, maybe because of some psychological strategy, because the guys looked at me and followed my gaze to the ball of paper, which I took advantage of to settle accounts with the leader, the darkest one. But the other two didn't lose a second in jumping on top of me, and why go into details? The truth is they kicked my ass worse than the time before, this time in earnest, along with every inch of my face.

WHEN JUAN LEFT THE ROOM I sat on the bed and started to cry. I thought I would never see him again. Then I chose the exact place where I would die: this room. My life was over at that moment. Suddenly someone opened the door. I could make out a silhouette.

28

Recovery

THE NEXT DAY I ached all over. Barbara was there and didn't stop talking. She had put a bandage on my head and some others on my body but I didn't even feel them. Like in a dream I watched her feed me.

"Juan, what the devil were you doing in the street at that hour? This is what you get for not telling me where you were going. And you didn't ask me for the car keys, either. The streets are dangerous: on every corner you have to watch out for the cars and the criminals. Now we have to stay here, for who knows how long. If your goal was to humiliate me, you succeeded. How can I take care of you when I don't feel well myself? Yesterday I had a terrible pain in my chest, but as usual, you never realized it. You pay no attention to me whatsoever. Your treatment costs money, too, sweetie, you better believe it. This morning I had to take out more money, we have almost nothing left. Everything is getting more and more expensive all the time. For God's sake! You can't even move after that beating those boys gave you last night."

Those boys again. That pissed me off because I knew that was Barbara's intention and I couldn't answer her back with my mouth all busted up.

"Eat it all up, please. Don't you know it's a sin to leave food in these times of crisis? What wonderful nights of no sleep and suffering I have in store for me! Ay, no, no! And it had to happen today of all days. Do you know what day this is?"

What would be the point of answering? Besides, I couldn't.

"Today is Mother's Day: May 10. What did I tell you? And what a nice present you've given me!"

Ah, her little jokes. I tried to say something with my mouth all swollen shut from the beating: "I can't hear you. Could you please be quiet? I'm dizzy."

But what I really meant was, "Don't give me any shit."

"I'll read your lips. After all this, I'm glad you taught me how to do it. Let's see, say it again?"

"Don't give me any shit!"

"Oh, you say you're very happy! Of course. That's the culmination of a love affair. We were born for each other! And now, eatupallyour soupIsaid..."

MUCH LATER I found a page she had torn out from the diary, folded, and stuck in the lining, which said:

DEAR DIARY: Poor Juan—he puts up with my senile ways...!

What a mystery: I realize that I have taken on my mother's most despicable behavior, and I can't avoid it. It's part of me; it's been hiding in some unknown recess of my body. On the other hand, how should I act? Like a wise old lover? It would be impossible for me to carry that off since I'm just now beginning to know what life is all about. I'm all spent, with no experience and no future. Besides, if I tried to play that character, I would die of exhaustion in a couple of hours. I wonder, now that we're stuck in this room for I don't know how many days, what can we do to entertain ourselves? If I were to let myself go, if I revealed who I really am at this moment, it would be absolute negation, nothingness. Juan would

leave after five minutes of seeing me lying in bed helpless against the
pain, suffering, bitter. That's why I cling to this role of mother and lover
at the same time, because it's less exhausting for me. All I have to do is
think of Mamá, and the words and attitudes come pouring out of their
own accord, as if they were sailing down that slide we had in the garden
when I was a child.

I READ IT much later on. At the time I just noticed that she left the
diary lying on the little table by the window where she had been
writing that afternoon.

Every morning she went out shopping. She set up a kitchen with
an electric hot plate and got food day by day so nothing would spoil.
Without a watch I lost track of the days and I had no idea how a
month went by. No one ever—no one had ever taken care of me—
good or bad—before… And certainly not like she did!

One day, when she had gone to buy some stockings, I managed to
stand up for the first time without any help. I made it to the window
and sat down at the table to look out at the street. There weren't
many people. It was Sunday. It was like a truce between Barbara and
the city, like they were giving each other time to recover. And I knew,
or I sensed, that the minute I got better, we would be back on the
streets again, and that this round was going to be the decisive one.

The diary was on the table, and since I didn't have anything to do,
I said, why not?

It was a book with no color on the outside. That must have been
because it was old. The pages were yellow and the ink was sort of a
coffee color. There was writing only about half way through, and the
rest was full of scratch outs and ink blots. There were also a lot of
blank pages. Maybe I would find out what my old lady was dying of.
I was interested. I started to flip through it. I found some dates, but
they were hard to decipher. And it didn't seem very orderly, you might

say. I think she only wrote in it when she felt like it or when she had
the chance. So she would probably open it at any page and just jump
in and write. If she'd taken the time to look for where she'd left off
last, the feelings would have faded away, and who wants to write only
the outline of their thoughts, right? Like going out in a downpour
with an umbrella that has no fabric, you know?

I always liked reading it because I understood her better that way
than I did in person.

I learned there that Barbara was in love with someone named Jorge.
That he was handsome and very smart. "*I love him,*" the diary said. *"I
absolutely adore him. He is a little older than I am, and the moment I
saw him I fell in love with him. Love at first sight came bursting into the
sitting room. I hadn't been alone with my mamá for very long when
suddenly there he was, standing by Papá's side. And Papá, my dear Papá,
was the one who introduced him to me. Buenos días, I said to him.*

"*Dear Diary, I have to go because my mamá just came upstairs and
I'm sure she's coming to say the rosary with me (or for me). I'm so happy!*

"*Dear Diary: Today I came home early from the Institute because he's
coming for lunch. I made the dessert with cream and strawberry jam. All
yesterday afternoon I was practicing the piano. Diós mío, I hope he doesn't
ask me to play for him! I think I would die.*

"*Dear Diary: Today he looked in my eyes for more than a minute,
although he was talking to me about something I didn't understand or
wasn't listening to.*

"*Though he didn't notice it, I blew him a kiss. But Mamá saw and she
got furious. Jorge is coming to pick me up from the Institute today. He
wants to talk to me. God help me!*

"*My heart is overflowing with joy. I went out with him. Papá gave
him permission to court me. If he only knew how much I love him!*

"*I'm absolutely furious. Papá is monopolizing Jorge. It seems he's got
some business with him.*

"Dear Diary, What in the world is 'the henriquismo movement'?

"Dear Diary! Dear Diary! Dear Diary! Today, at last, Jorge is down-stairs in the library talking with papá about something other than politics. I'm sure he is asking permission for us to be engaged. I'm sure that my dear papá will say yes. I...someone's coming upstairs... dear God!

"Forgive me for crying, but...I've never been so happy in my life. I'm the luckiest woman in the world. I feel ridiculous. I love him, I love him.

"Forgive me again for acting like a silly little girl. From now on I'm going to try to be a little more...ay, I don't know what word to use!...but I think I should be more reserved and not s...effusive in my displays of affection. I want my love to be proud of me. I will never disappoint him! Never. For me, Jorge is...ay, Jorge!...Jorge, Jorge, Jorge, Jorge, Jorge, Jorge, Jorge, Jorge, Jorge, Jorge, Jorge, Jorge, Jorge, Jorge, Jorge, Jorge, Jorge, Jorge, Jorge, Jorge.

"Dear Diary: There's no hope for me: I'm so corny...

"I have to tell you that I am now officially Jorge's fiancée. We're going to live in an apartment in the Hipódromo district. I'm sad, but I'm happy at the same time. I'm afraid...I don't know. Jorge doesn't want to tell me much about what's going on. I would like to console him. He'd have solace with me and I try to comfort him, but his problems are really worrying him, I know. But...I also know that he loves me.

"My mother scolded me because I held Jorge's hand in a restaurant downtown (that one with the tiles). There are a lot of things my mamá doesn't understand.

"Yesterday my father had a serious talk with me. He said that he has high hopes for me and I mustn't let him down. I'm going to be the wife

of one of the most important young politicians. I must do my best to be worthy of him. Dear Diary, I'm afraid.

"Today Jorge couldn't see me. He sent me a message saying that he had an urgent meeting with the party. I hope to God that there's nothing wrong."

AT THAT MOMENT I heard someone start up the Ford down below. I got scared. But then I saw Barbara look up from the street and blow me a kiss. Ever since that day, she did the same thing every morning so the engine wouldn't freeze up. I taught her that.

I heard her footsteps coming towards the room. I didn't have any more time to keep reading. Oh well.

29

The Thief

THAT AFTERNOON she told me she had gone to the supermarket, but she didn't have enough money with her, so she decided to steal the stockings.

"You—steal?"

"I never did it before, but at that moment it was necessary, Juan, something inexplicable, and very powerful. Very curious, isn't it?"

"And?"

"Well, what happened was that when I got there I realized I had left part of the money here, and it turned out that I didn't have enough, and I said to myself, 'I'm not going back without my stockings.' Then I put on the face of someone who wouldn't hurt a flea and without anyone noticing it, I put the pair of stockings in my purse. And off I go to the cash register. But then I look at a kid, one of those that you see everywhere, who was talking to a guy in a shirt and tie, another young man, about the same age as you. And then that one talked to the policeman at the door. 'Oh, man,' I said to myself, 'they've got me now.' And suddenly, quickly, I take the pair of stockings out of my purse and put in a baby's sleeper suit."

"A what?"

"A sleeper suit."

"But why?"

"I don't know. I saw it and liked it. Wait and let me finish what I'm telling you. So then I get to the cash register and I only pay for the stockings. Unfortunately I couldn't buy everything else I needed because I didn't have enough money, right? Okay, so I get to the cash register and I pay for the stockings. And then I head off toward the exit door with my heart about to jump out of my chest, like...later I'll tell you what I felt."

"What did you feel?"

"Ay, something very strange...I felt like—if I could steal something, no matter how little it was, I would sprout wings...no, it wasn't that. Let's see: okay, I felt powerful; I would no longer be hurt by any restriction; I would be able to break with total immunity all the NOs that exist on earth from the day we are born. I would gain...how can I explain it?...well, mobility, space, importance! And even if they threw me in jail I would still be free. I had never experienced that before. It was like some kind of jubilation, you know, but mixed with fear too, of course. Ay! It's something I will never forget, Juan!"

"Barbarita, you're hopelessly crazy," I said, totally shocked at those wild ideas that made her eyes shine so bright.

"Now, don't interrupt me or we'll be here all afternoon. I get to the door and the policeman blocks my way and I act like there's nothing wrong. 'Buenos días, señora,' he says to me. 'Buenos días,' I answer. 'Come with me, please.' 'Where to?' I ask. 'Just over here to the side.' 'What for?' I'm terrified, you understand. 'For you to show me what's in your purse,' he has the nerve to say to me."

"But how could you do that? Things have to be done right or they're just dumb-ass blunders."

"Don't be vulgar, Juan, please."

"Okay. Go on."

"Just wait till the end of the story. Then I stand up straight and a big scene starts to happen. Like 'If you will allow me.' 'I will not. Who do you think you're dealing with?' and all of that, I say. The people gathered around me. Then I really did get worried. 'I want to speak to your boss,' I say. And at that the manager shows up, the guy with the tie, along with the boy who saw me. 'I'm the manager.' And then I tell him, 'Look, this man is insinuating that I stole something or other.' And the policeman says, 'I was told I should detain her.' 'And who was the idiot who gave that order?' I say angrily, right? and the manager says to me, 'I did, because one of our employees saw you put a package of stockings into your purse.' And then that fool of a policeman says, 'Open your purse, please.' 'You keep quiet,' I say. 'Who is the one who saw me?' 'I am,' the boy says. So then I look him up and down and say to him, 'So you are the witness to my stealing something…? Well, you'd better state your full name because I am going to sue you for defamation of character.' The manager told me to control myself, he begged me to. The people kept milling around; some of them were laughing. I didn't really like that, but anyway, there was no way of turning back. And the manager says very seriously to me, 'Señora, please.' 'Señorita, if you please,' I answer. 'I beg you, calm down.' 'Well, no one likes to be taken for a thief, I'm sure you understand.' 'Come on, just open the purse'— it's the policeman again. And again I tell him to shut his mouth. 'Are you deaf, or what is the problem?' I say. 'I think that if you will show us the contents of your purse the problem will be over.' 'I…'"

"Who said that?"

"The manager, and I tell him, 'I'm not going to show anything. I want to speak to the owner of the supermarket.' 'What's the matter with you, señorita?' 'What is this you saw, little boy?' 'That you put some stockings in your purse.' 'Some stockings?' 'Yes, some stockings.' 'I know what stockings are,' I tell him, and then I say furiously,

'Here are your stockings, you little fairy'—I think that vulgar word came out because I've been living with you—and I pull out the stockings, but from the store bag, along with the ticket or whatever you call it, I mean, all paid for. Uy! Then the uproar really started. The people were indignant with the staff of the supermarket. There I was with the bag of stockings saying to the little squirt, 'Put them on, so you can learn better how to go around accusing innocent people.' Ay, can you believe it? How did I have the gall, Juan? 'Sure you saw it,' the manager says to the little squirt. 'I did see it,' the boy answered. I was about to die laughing but the policeman wouldn't give up. 'Well, show us what's in the purse anyway.' 'Very well,' I say, 'If you will tell me what it is I have stolen, I will open it.' He didn't know, of course. 'Then I won't open anything, and thank you very much for the *excellent* service, thank you.' 'You may go to any of the cash registers next week and your money will be refunded,' the manager said; but I answered him, 'I think I deserve at least an apology as well, don't you think?' 'Come on,' the manager said to the boy, and the poor boy had to apologize to me. 'I saw what I saw, but I'm sorry.' They gave me back the little slip of paper and the manager even gave me one of his cards in case I should have any problems in the future. Tomorrow I'll go and get the money. They'd better not think I'm going to wait a week. Life is too expensive. And then I heard the manager say to the boy, 'You're paying for those stockings, buddy.'"

30

Once Again, Guilt

THE NEXT DAY Barbara went to get the money back and left the sleeper suit with me, like she was putting me in charge of looking after our child. I read her diary again and went on from where I had stopped. I only had a little bit left to read before I finished it. That is, except for what she had added recently, but I had experienced all that with her, so why bother?

DEAR DIARY: I must be very sick now. My whole standard of behavior, so strict and limiting, has almost disappeared in these last days of my life. To begin with, I would never have allowed myself even the idea of having a lover, and now, it not only seems natural, but beautiful. What is happening to me? I love Juan just as he is, not in spite of his faults, but because of them. Yes, I love Juan, my chauffeur, who, because of his social class, would previously have seemed absolutely alien to me. But now, in spite of all that... It must be a miracle!

Now everything in this world seems understandable to me. Or rather: learning to accept that what can't be understood is the only thing real in human nature, has made me happy, and now that I'm happy I feel for the first time that I am truly a good person. I believe one cannot be 'good' if one is unhappy. Happiness is the antidote for evil. It isn't possible for someone who feels satisfied with himself to harm anyone else. My God, the things I'm saying…!

WELL, that had been written a few days ago, but when I turned the page, I found what I really wanted to read:

DEAR DIARY: At this point I don't know what is right or wrong. How I wish you could answer me. My father lent the Ford to Jorge. It obviously had something to do with Party business. But as I was leaving the Institute, Jorge came by to pick me up, without my parents having given me permission to ride with anyone who wasn't a member of the family, even if he weren't exactly a stranger. I got into the car before the astonished eyes of my girl friends. They were certain to gossip about it, but at that moment not anyone or anything in the world could stop me. We drove around all afternoon and I forgot to call home. Later Jorge stopped the car near a park and he kissed me. My God! He kissed me as he had never kissed me before. For the first time I felt the full weight of love. For a long time we sat like that, our heads close together, gazing at each other or closing our eyes and kissing. Later we laughed and laughed, I think we were out of control. At that moment I was the happiest woman in the world, but then…"

AND THE STORY ENDED. I was left in the middle of the orgasm. Maybe they told her what she was going to die of. Then I really did believe the old woman was hopelessly lost. It was true. But from what? Where was her old house, her father's house? Had she lost it? Didn't she have any family? Very little was written after something happened to her, and it didn't shed any light. It was very strange. Next came the things I already knew by heart, the ones she had written in front of me, as her chauffeur or her lover.

She got back late that day. She didn't even bring anything for me to eat. She didn't say a thing. She looked pretty bad to me. I asked her if she was sick and she said no. Like a jealous husband I demanded to know where she had been all day. "Did you go steal something else?" She shook her head and then she made supper for me.

I felt like the relationship between her and the diary was stronger than the one between Laura and me, or between my mother and me, or even between me and myself. We finished eating and she told me she was very tired and that the best thing for her was to sleep. We didn't watch television or make love. She just looked at me like no one had ever looked at me and caressed my whole body when she touched only my cheek.

I hadn't read her lips for a long time, I had forgotten all about it. I had learned to read other parts of her body better. But that time I couldn't learn anything. She was shut tight, with a calm face that seemed to be remembering the same past.

She helped me get into bed. At about four o'clock in the morning I opened my eyes. She was sitting at the little table by the window. The yellow light from the street illuminated her perfectly. She was writing in her diary and I only had a side view of her mouth. I had to use all my skill at lip reading to understand even half of her thoughts. It was like I had been robbed of one eye.

Then I realized that she was continuing what I had begun to read: *I must be very sick*, and all that, because she went on writing:

...IT'S A LIE: I'm not happy. Nobody can be! What does it matter if one breaks the rules established by common sense? In the marrow of our bones we are still whatever we were meant to be even before we were born... Once again guilt has cut its way into my heart, tearing me apart. And I cry in silence my bitterest tears..."

When I arrived at the church and sat down on the bench to wait for confession, my eyes suddenly grew cloudy and I heard only echoes. I made a tremendous effort and gained control of myself: I had to confess. Once again it was impossible for me to turn back. But you see, on the other hand…I had never done it before! It was all sick, diabolical. How can I say it? No, it wasn't all because of an impulse, dear Diary. It was, it was an overwhelming desire, a desire to fornicate, like a bitch in heat…

MY HEART understood first. I still didn't realize what was going on.

… TO THINK it could have been—as it was—that store manager or any other, whatever man who might have approached me. It was the right time and I… It's simply because I still half believe in the moral code I was taught, and this is what prevents me from making full sense. I am not happy, because I cannot be free.

I was more paralyzed by jealousy than if I had been clubbed on the head; if I hadn't been, I would have knocked the shit out of her. How could she have even tried to see some other man? Does she take me for her personal clown, or what? Laura was right: she would only need me for a little while.

I WAS TOO PISSED to read anything for a minute, but then:

…I CAN'T DECEIVE JUAN, nor myself, nor anyone else. I am sorry for my sins, and this is what I thought I'd say to the confessor: 'Father, I have been guilty since the day I was born. I have no salvation.' The feeling of guilt has been killing me throughout this lifetime. I am as guilty as I was on the day Jorge came by for me at the Institute and took me riding in the car. I will never be able to forget that afternoon. And a while ago, just a very short while, before Juan was beat up, when I remembered my mother because of the chance meeting with my friends, I got into the car and told Juan to go faster, to race faster and faster, and the wind blew away the memory of my mother and it brought me Jorge's caresses in the car, like

the ones of that other time, when I felt pleasure for the first time in my life! I thought of nothing but my love for Jorge, of giving myself to him until the passion had consumed me. But then they caught us, and it was them, my father's loyal friends, they saw to it that my reputation was soiled. Guilt for the first time. Sin, just like today when I deceived Juan by sleeping with another man. I felt the same. Dirty, as with Jorge. I no longer have my father, may he rest in peace, but I need him today to wound me again, to stop me and to castrate me once and for all. What terror freedom inspires in me…!

At that time he said horrible things to me. I was the hope of the family, whose fortunes had been falling ever since my grandfather lost everything in the Revolution, and I had dishonored them. My father humiliated me for having given in to Jorge's caresses, even though he knew that it had been nothing more than that—caresses. My name began to grow bigger and bigger in the city that was becoming smaller all the time. I was very frightened. Rejected by the world, I would have to live a life of eternal loneliness. But not just I; I had soiled my whole family so that they would never be able to survive the shame.

One day, after a terrible tirade, my father felt an unbearable pain in his chest. At that moment I realized that I was a murderer and imposed on myself a life sentence of fears and anxieties. When I felt the urge to help him, someone knocked at the door. It was Jorge. He came to save me, because despite all the vicious rumors, he loved me. I remember his words: 'I'll marry her and quiet all the whispering against our love.' He was the prince, the hero, the savior, the 'only' man in the whole universe who could love me. And everything changed. The shadows disappeared. My mother and I planned the ceremony in the Iglesia de San Agustín. Our friends were amazed at all we did. I was going to show them that I had overcome impropriety. My father had no further health problems. We bought the wedding dress at one of the best clothing stores on Insurgentes Centro. It was white, as was fitting…

It was a very short-lived dream, and for it I paid and continue to pay a price that even today, even though I know it's disproportionate, I cannot stop paying. The blissful time lasted a few weeks. Since then more than forty years have gone by. What insanity! Forty years... Someone inside me watches my memories as if they were a film with Greta Garbo...

When it was my turn, I told the priest I had stolen a sleeper suit, and nothing more. The penance he gave me wasn't much.

BARBARA CLOSED her diary without mentioning the great shame of her life. Or had she already mentioned it? But in the end she married Jorge because he loved her, he told her that, didn't he? So then? At the end I had to confess too, to myself, that I didn't understand a damn thing.

She sat there at the window, watching the street without seeing it. Silent. I sensed that she was far away because she had become lost in oblivion. Even if I reached out my hands, even if I ran to her, I could never ever reach Barbara. It was foolish to even try. The strange thing is that the jealousy left me as if by magic, even though I still felt manly. And so I got up from the bed and went to her; I lifted her by the shoulders and I screwed her.

DEAR DIARY: My life was on hold while Juan's injuries were healing. The city agreed to wait for me; it was as if it were some secret pact between two ladies who feel mutual respect. We set our hatreds aside for a moment and we each felt an enormous vacuum that united us. But one day Juan was better. I knew it because it was the first time in a long time that he made love to me.

31

My Way

NOW IT'S MY TURN.

She had already had her chance. Now she was going to do every-thing the way I wanted. Okay? That's how it was going to be. She wanted to die in the city? No problem. Let her die. But you better believe it would be done my way. We made a deal. Whoever can't hack it is a chickenshit. I told her, "Look, Barbara, you took care of me and all that, right?—but now we're going to have our fun when and where I say so, okay?"

She didn't even look at me; she just smiled. She knew I was look-ing at her mouth and so she didn't risk saying anything.

She bought clothes for me; she didn't steal them. Just the kind I liked. We spent more time at the hotel while I was fixing the Ford up real cool: I added four more rear view mirrors. One of them was as big as the windshield. The Virgencita de Guadalupe of course—hooked up to the battery so she could light us up with her aura of punk rays—was glued tight in place above the radio with resistol. There wasn't enough money for a stereo, because if there had been… Another crucifix was hanging from the support of the rear view mir-ror. Shag carpeting all over to make it cozier and, as they say, more comfortable. I didn't hang up my baby shoes because I had lost them.

I also started plastering the dash with pictures and decals of Pedro (Infante, of course), Isela Vega and Los Tigres del Norte. The antenna that followed the curve of the humpback was totally cool. On the hood, I put the mermaid of the seven seas with her tits to break the wind and her butt for me to look at. Since you can't get halogen bulbs any more, I put yellow filters over the headlights. The chrome had to go. All smooth. Cherry!

Barbara watched it all from the hotel window. She would go back into the room and come to the window again. I'm sure she was writing something in her diary.

Finally it was ready and I told her it was time. She came down like a queen about to enter her new home.

THAT SAME NIGHT we left the hotel to return to the world. Something told me it was for the last time. Juan was uncontrollable and I didn't really care much about anything anymore. He wanted to have his fortune read in the cards; they told him he would die on Tuesday the 13th. The calendar stopped there for him. They told him it would be wise not to leave the house on that day. 'Don't get married or set out on a trip or leave your woman's side.'

I suddenly felt curious to know what was left of my fate, and the cards came out saying I would live many happy peaceful years surrounded by my grandchildren. It made me laugh and I kissed Juan on the lips. The fortuneteller just about fainted.

I TOLD BARBARA we would go to the wrestling matches first and to please not make me do anything ridiculous. She blew me away when she said she had always wanted to go, but that it had been more than impossible. She really wanted to see Tarzán López and Tonina Jackson fight. God knows who those monkeys could have been.

On our way to the arena another wave of nostalgia came over her.

Then I had to go the whole way out there listening to how she used to go to the Cine Rex to see the Esther Williams films. Then she got off on bull fights, and then how she wanted to meet Pepe Ortiz. Then we got onto the theme of XEW again and then she told me that when she would get out of school early she used to go see Luis G. Roldán, and she started singing again: "Perfidia," and "Vuelve Por Favor," "Humanidad" and all those atrocious old songs. She said that her mother said it was good to listen to the radio a lot because sound waves are good for the scalp. Something like a massage. She knew commercials from Methuselah's day and then she asked me if I used to entertain myself by learning commercials by heart. I said I didn't. And then she came out with the stupid question of whether I had had a happy childhood. I figured it was best not to answer, and she just started singing commercials: "When you drink more than you ought, you need something to pick you up, a glass filled to the top with Sal de Uvas Picot. How tasty: Sal de Uvas Picot. Doctors prescribe it for children and everybody else. I always carry it in my pocket and take it all the time for almost every problem…" "¡Sister Engracia, the milk is boiling over! Forgive me, Reverend Mother, I was choosing the almonds, the cinnamon and the vanilla, weighing the sugar and counting the eggs. Then we have everything ready to make some delicious crema de Rompope Santa Clara. I'm going to the choir loft and I'll be back…" "Pepsi Cola, everyone drinks Pepsi Cola, because they know it gives them so much more. Pepsi Cola, delicious. More, more in each bottle. Yes, yes it tastes better. More, more in each bottle. With Pepsi Cola you get twice as much. Remember, don't let yourself be confused by all those colas…" "Wife, wash my clothes with Uno Dos Tres soap…"

"That's enough!" I howled.

At last we got to the Arena México. You could hear the shouting even from outside; she got excited.

Once we got there things got better. At first Barbara didn't seem to like it, but then later she got so worked up that I had to duck because if I hadn't she would have broken my jaw again with a perfect right. I had a bottle of tea of quila. "Take a chance," I said. I don't think it could have tasted good to her because this was the first time she had drunk it, and especially from the bottle, but she didn't even notice because she was so into the fights. Barbara sucked it down like all get out, better than any old woman you ever saw.

Between one round and another I showed her how to smoke, because she didn't know how. And her smoke mixed in with the collective cloud that covered that place.

I FOLLOWED JUAN in everything he did. It's incredible how the will can overcome fatigue... It's also true that I enjoyed myself, but the joy was angry, brutal. And now I realize that I only did it so I would get my compensation before it was too late: I longed for... had always longed for a love like the one that was cut short in Jorge. I wanted a romantic spot. I desperately needed so much tenderness! Where could I find the magic that makes your eyes shine, that makes your hands tremble like in the movies? Ay, dear Diary, time really does exist in us, and because it's so short it's so imperceptible...! I'm fifteen years old again, my God...! Pathetic. But then, will I die without having fulfilled this dream...? And Juan...? Yes, he will die without dreams too, as alone as I am.

Many years ago a friend assured me that we are all islands. Once in a while, another island travels along with us for a short stretch, and then it goes away, it slips off to some other place, and we never see each other again. Life is nothing more than a system of good-byes. Of releases. Of mutilations. The truth is we are incapable of giving anyone what they really need.

One day I told Juan about the romantic place. He promised to take me to a perfect place for love. I imagined a wheat field where the wind makes everything go slow.

He took me to Chapultepec Park. First there was the problem of getting there and finding a parking place for the car. Then there were so many people. My God! We ended up sitting on patches of grass, in the middle of scraps of food and dog filth. Juan was asleep, and I at his side surrounded by children playing. That was all. When I got up so we could go, finally! at last! thank God! I had lost my adolescent dreams forever.

THEN I let her twist my arm: she wanted to go to the country or something like that. I took her to Chapultepec Park. She was really happy.

The third day I took her to the Colonia Dance Hall, the one with the big black face with its mouth open, a mouth that never said anything. She told me her father had scolded her when he caught her dancing the mambo, because it was the music of savages and animals. But now the old lady was taking flight, and I let her. The goddamn bitch even danced better than me and you can bet I used to hang around that place a lot back when I was picking up the dance hall girls. And that's not all: a couple of times she left me high and dry while the goddamn woman danced with one of the regulars. We also had a bottle with us and I really got her shit-faced. We were the last ones to leave, singing, "A lost woman you have been branded. In this life betrayed and abandoned, with no love to offer you hope. A lost woman, because you dragged yourself down after you shattered and threw to the ground what virtue and honor you had. I don't care if you say I am lost." That's not how the song went; it went, I don't care if you say *you are lost*, not if you say *I am lost*.

"I am?" I said.

"I am what?" And the stubborn woman sang again: "I don't care if you say I am lost."

Suddenly the old lady blurted out her postal zip code, and since we were drunk to the point of "I can't remember anything any more" we started to die laughing—but it was that kind of laughter that comes more from your guts than from yourself. You don't have any air left, just bad breath with a sense of humor.

We got to the Ford still laughing. I took out the keys somehow, I think from my shorts, wet from laughing, and I couldn't get it into the hole. That made us laugh even more. All of a sudden she gave the car a kick and said, "Open up, you fucking old wreck."

She had never said a single dirty word before. We split our sides laughing.

"So, now it's *fucking* and all the rest, huh?" I managed to say.

"And its mother too," she answered, laughing so hard she was crying.

"And its father?" I kept up the joke.

"That one is strictly high class, the son of a bitch," the old lady blurted out. And right there she started to pee from laughing so hard and left a big puddle on the ground. I started pounding the Ford, nearly choking from laughter when I heard the *chipi chipi* of her pee.

"You're out of control," I returned. "Aren't you about ready to de-liver the...goods?"

"Yes, but all peed on," she finished, sitting on the sidewalk with her legs spread and soaked. Her face, which was squinched as much as it could be, turned into an enormous scar.

I managed to get the door open and when I did out fell the *Manual of Courtesy and Good Manners*. We shit our pants laughing. We left it there.

"The things that fall out of this car..."

"So...?"

"What?"

"What about that Jorge?" I remembered the name from her diary, but she thought I said, "What about that Ford?"

"Oh, yes. I rented it out."

"You rented him?" I said dying of laughter. "Jorge?" She couldn't even hear me.

"For weddings and fifteenth birthday parties."

"For weddings and fiftee...! I can't stand it! Hahahaha...I said 'Jor...ge!'"

"Jorge?"

The laughter stuck in her gizzard and suddenly she couldn't breathe. A catch in my own heart dried up my laughter too.

"Damn, it's impossible to have a good time with you because you always feel bad. Don't you see? You've ruined everything. Stop coughing. It was just a joke. The thing is we're just not in the same league. I can take more than you. You'd better accept that and not go around with big ideas about how you can handle everything. So watch what you do, or you're going to stay in the hotel and I'll go out alone. Are you listening to me?"

She didn't answer me, I guess because she was coughing so much she couldn't hear.

I found her diary and pretended to write, reading it to myself with a woman's voice.

"I FOLLOWED JUAN in everything he did. It's curious..."

I RAISED MY EYES to meet Barbara's. They had a look—how can I say it?—gentle; her open mouth drew in a little air and made a rasping sound like a death rattle. For an instant we stayed looking at one another without breathing. Then she relaxed, she was calm, she closed her mouth and began to grow pale until her face was all a light blue.

I was filled with anger, against who I don't know. I started the car up with a jerk. The anger only left me when we entered the hotel and her body felt like it was made of feathers, light as could be. Because of that I almost lifted her off the ground and carried her to the room. I think it made me feel tender…

I put her to bed there. She looked like a little girl who was waiting for her good-night kiss. Damn it! And didn't I feel like I was her papá?

An hour went by. The blue was fading to reveal her wrinkles. Now she was a little old lady. Then she moved. She put her hands to her head and smoothed her hair. She made a face, like in disgust.

Then she sat up in the bed. Her voice was that of a strong, drunken woman. "How do I look? I'm almost sobered up already, as drunk as we were."

"What are you saying?"

"I want to go on partying," she said and stood up. She went to the mirror.

"And what do you think we've been doing all this time?" I answered, pissed off. "You're the one who ruined everything with that little coughing fit of yours… Listen, baby, do you want to?"

"You won't keep up with me till morning." And she turned toward me, challenging me.

You won't keep up with me till morning! I never dreamed she'd say something like that. "No. I don't want to because then you'll get sick and…"

"Just this last time. I promise you the next time I really will die."

32

Get Even, Juan! Go For It!

I DON'T KNOW WHY I chose the streets around where I picked her up the first time in my taxi. And we took the same route to her house there in the Santa María la Ribera district, as if the same thing was happening again. It started to rain and she fogged up the window with her breath. And she was wearing black as usual, like she had been wearing the first time too. Again she started talking fast with her lips, but this time I didn't understand her. Everything repeated itself and I didn't know how. Or was everything just about to happen? I became illiterate in my own specialty. This time I felt lonely, unsure of myself. I didn't know where she was directing me, like the time by San Agustín. She was the one who had everything to gain. I felt like once again and forever things were going to be done her way. I didn't speak. Only Barbara knew what she was thinking. Not even God.

We drove close to her house, which I had taken her from more than a couple of months ago, or even more, ever since my watch had been stolen and we went crazy…

The house was already occupied again. The car that was in the garage was also old, the same as mine, but in bad shape. Barbara didn't even turn and look at her old house. I slowed down from forty to twenty but nothing happened; we went on and I sped up to fifty and in the four rear view mirrors I saw everything we had passed.

We went on down the same street. Then she told me to turn to the right, then to the left, then straight ahead and we came to what was originally a big house, I think, but now it had been converted into a restaurant for tourists or something like that… She had me park the car across the street from it. She got out with the bottle in her hand and looking all filthy and beat up. I didn't have to read any part of her to know what she was going to do to one of the big windows, where on the other side a couple of old gringos were eating dinner.

I got out of the car the best I could to help her not break the glass. I don't remember exactly what we said, but the old folks figured out what was happening—myself, I wasn't so sure. I couldn't get the bottle away from her. Everything turned to rubber on me and I slipped. She went up to the window and the old people called for the maitre d', but there didn't seem to be one. Then I heard the glass breaking to pieces, which started falling right beside me. I grabbed her and got her back into the Ford. I just had time to turn and see the last piece of window glass dangling there like a guillotine. I think it fell as we were leaving. The waiters came out to catch us, but with the Ford, how could they?

Running all the stop signs, protected by the saint of taxi drivers, which she probably would say didn't exist, all I saw were the avenues flying past, echoing with the sound of horns.

"You're crazy!"

"Why? Didn't you want to have a good time? Well, then."

"You're ready for the old farts' home, I think."

"Now you're the one who's spoiling all the fun."

"This isn't fun."

"Coward."

"Your mother."

"Fucking coward. Faggot. Do something to match it!"

Now her swearing was terrible. It tore at my soul. I couldn't stand to hear her talking that way.

"You're the one who won't keep up till morning."

"I'm getting tired of this."

"You don't know me."

"What a shame, coward."

"Shut up!"

"Come on. It's your turn now. Get even! Let's see you, Juan! You can't do it, can you?"

"I'm going to give you a dick whipping—that'll shut you up."

"All you know how to do is run stop signs; that's as much as you dare to do. Uy! How scary! There goes another one…ooh, how awful!"

Suddenly I hit the brakes and practically smashed her face, just like the other time, when she was my boss. I saw her; she was still challenging me with all her body. And then she shook her head slightly like she was saying *fucking fag*. Well, maybe what she said was *You should be ashamed*, but for me it was *fucking fag*. I shifted into first and headed for Laura's apartment.

Barbara stayed inside the Ford, and there I was with my finger on the doorbell. When Laura poked her head out the window, I was already six motherfuckers ahead of her.

SEVERAL DAYS have gone by and now Juan is the one who follows my lead. Ever since the cards told him he had no future, he seems more and more like me.

"COME DOWN HERE, Laura. Come down, you fucking bitch, and see who it is you're fucking with."

"You're drunk. Get out of here. I don't want to know anything about you."

"Come down, bitch."

The neighbors came out, or something like that. What mattered to me was Barbara, the rest didn't mean a damn thing. I turned toward her, as if to say, *So how's that?*

"Come down."

"Get out of here."

"Come down and make me if you can."

Now she didn't do anything, she just went into her room. But first she nodded her head, like she was saying she was coming down. Okay. I was waiting there to let her have it under the chin, but instead of her the one who appeared was the big gorilla who had smashed my eye in the VIPS. I turned toward Barbara and she was smiling; she seemed to be saying, *This is when we find out, you little fairy.*

I looked back at the guy who was screwing my ex, and I gave him a kick in the balls that left him doubled up in pain. Yes!

I got back into the Ford and took off. The damned woman didn't even congratulate me or anything. She just said, "Okay, the game's over for us. Let's go back to the hotel."

No way! Too easy. I had to follow this through to the end. This couldn't stop again just because she said so. The rat was off and running; fuck the goddamn cat. Besides, I was really enjoying this business of getting even. Before I knew her, I had lived the life of "every so often," not even the life of "today," but now she had shown me how to figure up everything that was owed to me. And it was a whole fucking lot!

But she was all "Let's go to the hotel. Come on. Right now, Juan." She said it as if she had broken something. As if she was satisfied with her little revenge. I had barely begun. We were at odds again, but I didn't care. I had learned the sweet taste of rage and now, like a vampire, I'm after your blood, fucking Life!

Since I was the one behind the wheel she had no choice but to go along with me. Now she wasn't saying anything. She slumped down in the seat, and I walked my butt forward to get closer to the windshield.

33

Barbara!
Where Are You?

TAKING THE CORNER at five kilometers an hour, I parked the car with the lights off so that they wouldn't see me. I told Barbara not to get out and to just watch what I was going to do. From the trunk I took a knife and a can of spray paint I had bought a long time before. To use some day.

There was no one in México Park. It was nighttime and I was alone. The light was on in the taxi booth of my ex-buddies, the drivers. Four cars sat there waiting and the drivers were in the booth watching TV. My ribs trembled and my laughter made them chirp like crickets; my God, how I wanted to do this! I got to the first taxi. I slashed a tire, and while the car tipped to the side all by itself, I masturbated with the can of paint and shot red come all over the doors: pinches putos. I came about four times on the trunks of their cars, until another taxi arrived and its lights caught me there like a pervert. I ran to the Ford while the guy got out hollering. The guys in the booth came running out to chase me. "It's Juan," one of them shouted. "We'll kick his fucking ass," came from another.

I got in the car. I blinded them with my lights, and then I started talking to myself, because when I turned around, I didn't see Barbara.

"Stupid! I told you not to get out!"

I got out of the car; I'd totally lost it. "Barbara! Barbara!"

I looked through the trees and didn't find her. They were getting close and I was shouting, "Barbara!" I went back to the car and blew the horn. "Barbara!" They were right on top of me and I took off. I drove around the park, but I couldn't find her. I couldn't find her. I couldn't find her. My God! I came around the curve again doing five kph and I saw that they were taking Barbara into the taxi booth. I didn't even think about it. I pressed the gas pedal, I pressed it, I wanted to leave, but a part of me kept saying no, I had the clutch down and I couldn't let it out, and another part of me was pressing the gas pedal, and another part holding the clutch, and I sat there like that, like I was two people. Puta madre! What the motherfucking hell should I do? And then it just happened, my foot slipped off the clutch pedal and I flew against the taxi booth and *bam*! I saw one guy go flying and Barbara thrown to one side. I got out and slugged one guy and gave another a kick, and then I picked up Barbara to put her back in the car. One guy in the booth wasn't moving. Now I was a murderer! I didn't know. I didn't care about anything. I took off.

Barbara was in bad shape and I repeated, "To the hotel, yes, to the hotel." At ten kilometers per hour, and then at twenty, and then at thirty, and at forty, and at sixty and at eighty and at ninety. I kept saying to myself that nothing would have happened if I had just paid attention to her. "Everything's going to be fine; yes, everything will work out; you'll see. It's all right now."

The car stopped for some reason. An accident up ahead, I don't exactly remember what, there in the Centro. Barbara looked out her window at a tamale vender that she confused with Death, and she stuck out her tongue at her. Then she started to sing. The last straw! "Tamales for sale, tamales of chile and grasshoppers, nice and hot and ready to eat." Then came the ambulance for the dead people from the wreck up ahead. I didn't know what other street to take. The tamale vender took a piece of meat from her steaming pot and offered it to Barbara. A bunch of kids in their underwear shouted at her, "Here comes the witch. Here comes the witch." I figured out a way to get out of there and we were ripping ass again.

34

The Last Time in the Hotel

WE JUST GOT INTO THE ROOM and we started going at it in bed. No one said anything. We didn't even ask if we wanted to. We did it until dawn because at this point we weren't leaving anything out. She did it like she was about to die.

She went into the bathroom first. She came back to bed while I was smoking a cigarette. Then I got up and went to wash myself.

In there I saw spots of blood floating in the toilet and also in the sink.

"Barbara...! There's blood in here...! What's wrong with you? What's happening?"

She looked at me and without even reacting she covered her face with the sheet.

"Something's broken inside you and you didn't tell me about it. And you made love like that?"

She laughed underneath the sheet.

"I did it, didn't I? I broke something in you, Barbara, with the car in the taxi booth. Was it me? Tell me."

She didn't say anything. She just let the blame fall on me slowly, and in silence.

"I just wasn't thinking. It was the only thing I could think to do at the moment. Do you understand me? Run the car into them, kill them, I don't know. You're bleeding, Barbara, what's wrong? What did I do to you? Does it hurt?"

She answered me coldly, "No. Not anymore. Get in bed and stop thinking about it."

"Son of a bitch! Because of me…"

"Come on."

I went.

"But what about you? Why did you leave the car? I told you to stay."

"So now it's my fault? Is that what you're trying to tell me?"

I think it was because I couldn't think of any words that I moved up against her, and I hugged her, wanting to do it again. And she was cold, not saying a word. But I could turn her on any time I wanted.

"How does it feel to make love with a worn-out old bag?"

I practically jumped out of the bed.

"Don't jack me around!"

"Tell me!"

"You sure know how to turn someone off."

"Why? I just want to know if what excites you is that you're sleeping with a woman who's practically dead. Is that it? You're morbid?"

"Morbid?"

"Yes. Admit it: that's why you stay with me."

"No… Okay, the real truth is I don't know why I stay with you. I think…"

"Don't hold anything back. Say it. What does it feel like to do it with someone who is starting to die?"

"Well…strange, real strange."

"But you like it."

"…I don't know. Why are you asking me all this?"

"Just a premonition, perhaps."

"Of what?"

"Ay, I shouldn't tell you this…just go on making love to me instead. It could be the last time."

"Right now?"

It was so hard, for me at least, to go on screwing after talking about death and how everything is coming apart. I made an effort to concentrate and said, "Well, I've already seen a lot of things with you, and one more…"

I started to kiss her again, but then again I stopped cold.

"Have you ever started thinking that death could be in the look of the person you have beside you?"

"Okay, enough. Shut up about it, please."

"I feel like maybe you…you're going to go with me, Juan."

"You're talking bullshit."

"I'm telling you it's a premonition."

"Well, you can fry your premonition to a chicharrón."

"And how can you be so sure it won't be like that, eh? Who can guarantee you that my disease isn't contagious? And what if you already have it?"

She put one finger in her mouth; a thread of saliva dangled from her lips to the finger nail when she took it out. She put the finger in my silent, terrified mouth. Then she lowered it to the level of my heart and then slid it down to my dick, and that was when I felt it. I moved to the side without taking my eyes off her.

"How do you know you won't go to the bathroom some day and find blood and be so sick that you can't recognize whether it's your blood or mine?"

She pulled me toward her, but I stopped her. She was stronger than anyone could have imagined, but I stopped her.

"Don't mess with this business of predictions; that's serious stuff, I'm telling you. What do you have? If you're going to die, that's you, but why me? You almost died already, do you know that?"

"Maybe you're right. After all, I never could catch up with life, I ran alongside it, parallel to it, and because of that I could never climb on and ride. I only managed to tire myself out. And it got away from me; and so it's not so terrible to die. Are you afraid, Juan?"

"It's not that."

"You're afraid."

"I said I'm not."

"Do you love me?" It was the only time she asked me that. I got up, disgusted with hating myself so much.

"Where are you going?"

I went into the bathroom. I was scared. I wet my face with my mouth still open. I didn't know exactly what was happening to me. Then I no longer thought about why I didn't go away and leave her to die alone. I looked at the white floor and saw a bloody footprint beside me. I walked backwards and the footprints followed me until I smashed up against the wall with my mouth gaping wide open. I slid down the tiles to the floor and the blood was up to my feet.

35

As Pale as a Magnolia

AFTER THAT NIGHT, when I slept with her scabs under my finger-
nails, we never spoke much again. I had a dream in which I saw the
car without its body. I saw broken hoses flooding my mouth with oil
that gargled in my throat. The fan had broken blades and the fuel
lines sprayed gasoline. The overheated engine burned my skin.

We left the hotel for the last time and packed everything we could
into the old Ford. This time I didn't ask her where to go, and she
didn't say anything. I started the engine and the car slid out rattling
loudly all over.

We drove along the same streets as before, without direction, staring out the windshield. Time passed away: I don't know if it was
days, months or years. The money ran out and the little we could get
went for gasoline. And then there wasn't even any for that, and we'd
take off without paying, ripping the hose from the gas pump. For a
gas cap we used our baby—the sleeper suit—and little by little the
car got older and more foolish.

Inside, it was like an abandoned insane asylum: full of rags and
pieces of rotten food and even urine. The windshield clouded over

with the fumes of the city, and of us inside. I couldn't see very well, just things that moved about with horrible faces. Sometimes we would drive up and down the same lonely street, in forward and reverse. The aura fell from the Virgencita de Guadalupe, and the Cristo hanging from the rear view mirror had one loose arm that banged constantly against the windshield. Cold weather came and I put on the chauffeur's cap and jacket, stained with blood from the ass-kicking the kids had given me. Once, you could hear chains breaking when we were heading toward the exit for Cuernavaca. I saw the highway, which was what I had been wanting to take all along, to get out of there; but I was given this opportunity when it no longer mattered to me.

I had discovered my most lowdown things with Barbara, and just when I was letting them burn, once again there was that feeling of inconclusive screwing, because now we were constantly moving, totally outside of time, everything going so fast, that I didn't even have a chance to tell myself exactly what was happening.

Suddenly the car lurched to the right and I stopped thinking what I had been thinking, and the car kept swerving more and more to the right until I stopped it and the tires screeched on their own toward the same direction.

When Barbara wiped the windshield with her little hand, we realized that in front of us stood a statue dedicated to the people who build highways, and that the street folded up to become a wall. We just stayed there for a while, looking at how the road twisted. I think it was raining, but who knows. I only remember that I followed that white line and thought about many things. I don't know if I read it on her lips or in her diary or whether I had always known it, I don't remember, but I saw Barbara, like in a movie from the '40s, waiting for the rest of her friends outside her old house, next to the car wrapped like a present, for her wedding, like when I saw it for the first time.

She is very young and pretty in her new dress for her farewell to the single life. Other guests are there, and her mother nearby and her father speaking to the chauffeur, but I didn't notice exactly who the driver was. Suddenly another car of exactly the same year pulls up and a guy jumps out running and shouting: "They killed them. They killed them. They killed Jorge. It happened on Avenida Juárez, at the Hemiciclo. All hell has broken loose on Juárez. They killed everyone in the Alameda. Lots of people are dead."

Jorge is dead... whispers pass among the guests...something like *the movement is finished. The Party is destroyed. Poor girl. The henriquismo movement has been blown all to hell*—something like that.

The white line doesn't leave me. Then Barbara wrings her little hands and refuses to believe it. And then her father says, "It's your fault, it's your own stupid fault that your mother and I are ruined. Look at what you've done to us! He's dead, there's no one else. Now NO ONE WILL EVER LOVE YOU. NOW YOU'LL NEVER BE ABLE TO MARRY ANYONE. NEVER." And she suffers terribly. For being a whore. Because she was caught one time in a car, with the wind between her legs. Because Jorge was her last chance, because from before she was born, Barbara had been condemned to play a role in a film that would leave her crying forever. Because her father wanted to go on living but she killed him with sheer mortification. For that? Just for that? Forty years like this, just for that?

I saw everything perfectly clearly with the white line. Later I couldn't see any more because it stopped raining. I shifted into reverse and we went back toward everything that was still suspended in time.

She said, "Juan, fill the tank for the last time."

I filled it, but everything was being used up at a thousand kilometers an hour. And suddenly, from full, the gas gauge dropped down to three quarters. I dropped the speed from seventy to fifty and the needle showed a half a tank. I dropped down to forty, and the needle went from a half to a quarter. Then I drove at thirty. I was panting like a thirsty dog. Anxiety. Maybe if I went slow it would last longer; yes, of course.

When the needle reached the red reserve zone, I didn't want to go on any further. Spin the wheel to win more life. At last I could feel strongly, without a doubt, that I didn't want her to die! I didn't want her to die!

The car started to jerk, and because of that Barbara's life was going out of her. She was in her death agony. I stopped the car on a hill near the Circuito, in the San Rafael district, and I got into the back seat where she was dying in the night.

"I know nothing is going to happen. I know it. Listen, we've done a lot of stupid things, but we won't do them anymore—we're going to live, Barbara. You're not going to leave me now that you've finally taught me how to remember, right? Come out of it, for God's sake! Barbara! Listen to me!"

There was no air left in her; she was deflated.

"Aha!" she whispered, "That's good…"

"You're about to see that miracles happen."

"Ay, Juan…not that…"

She suffered, she still suffered greatly in dying. But then, suddenly, she opened her eyes, she smiled and regained her beauty and youth. She was gorgeous, more than anyone I had ever seen. Even her voice sounded liked a young girl's.

"I want to remember a…an ending of a movie…and I can't do it." A little laugh. "I can't do it…I've got to remember it!"

"How can I help you? What should I do? I don't even remember."

"Put on some music…to create…atmosphere…"

I managed to get to the front seat and turned on the radio. The first thing we heard was the National Hymn. I switched stations and the Hymn was still playing, and on another and another and on all of them they were playing the National Hymn.

"Puta madre! It's the National Hour! Barbara!"

When I got back to her she was already dead. She had died, the bitch, and I wasn't there. I didn't see it. She must have said something because her mouth was open... Much later I realized that she had sent me a kiss.

Pinche vieja, why did you leave like that? And then out of me came the word and all the words that never had meant anything, not to her nor to her Diary. And it was easy for me, more than easy, it was urgent that I tell her that I loved her. I said it to her right in front of her open eyes, like this: "Barbara, I love you." I moved my mouth closer and repeated it so that she could see, I told her with my lips: *I love you.* Understand it, Barbara! Let the last bit of life you have in you peer out of your eyes and see my mouth telling you that I love you. And I kissed them.

I WAS REALLY TIRED. I couldn't breathe either. I started the car and went lurching out onto the Circuito. And there the old car died for good, along with her, surrounded by chaos.

IN THE CINE REX we all listened to Lara's song, all of us, because now it was my movie too.

All that was left of the afternoon and of your oath, was the fleeting sensation of a kiss that can never return. The fleeting sensation of a kiss that can never return.

I listened to it all the way through to give Barbara the romantic moment she had fought me for so often. Then I got out of the Ford and walked, breaking through the spider web of trapped cars that screamed like wounded animals. Then I turned back toward the Ford: it had turned into a black hole, a hole that hurt and into which my life was beginning to slide.

I could never remember the dream, but I could remember what I thought before going to sleep: I was a hurt dog, on an empty street, late at night, licking its wounds one by one without thinking about anything.

THEN I DISAPPEARED on some unnamed corner of this city. Of this city.

Luis Eduardo Reyes

is a prize-winning playwright, a writer
for film and television, and a novelist.
This is his first book to be translated into English.
Originally from Guadalajara, Reyes now lives
and works in Mexico City.

OTHER CINCO PUNTOS PRESS BOOKS
FROM THE BORDER
& FROM MEXICO

The Moon Will Forever Be a Distant Love
by Luis Humberto Crosthwaite
(translated by Debbie Nathan and Willivaldo Delgadillo)

The Late Great Mexican Border
Reports from a Disappearing Line
edited by Bobby Byrd and Susannah Mississippi Byrd

Women and Other Aliens
Essays from the U.S./Mexico Border
by Debbie Nathan

Ghost Sickness
poems by Luis Alberto Urrea

Dark and Perfect Angels
poems by Benjamin Alire Sáenz

Eagle-Visioned/Feathered Adobes
poems by Ricardo Sánchez

For more information or a catalog, contact:

CINCO PUNTOS PRESS
2709 Louisville
El Paso, TX 79930
1-800-566-9072